# FALLOUT

## BURNING SKIES
### BOOK 2

## JACQUELINE DRUGA

# VULPINE

## PRESS

Published by Vulpine Press in the United Kingdom in 2018

Cover by Claire Wood

ISBN: 978-1-912701-14-8

www.vulpine-press.com

To my daughter Veronica, for all the nights you had to sit and listen to me work out this story and for all your feedback, I dedicate this book to you.

# CHAPTER ONE

## Cleveland, Ohio

Harris Clemmons watched the world end on a ten-inch monitor screen from the second subbasement floor of Kobak, Stewart, and Lane Securities. It wasn't hard to miss. He was watching for it. People running, an abundance of interference on his screens, a distant flash, then nothing.

Now he sat in a room built for such an event.

Twenty-four hours had passed.

Harris was alone. He didn't need to be. That was something he grappled with.

He had worked security there and had done so for six years. He usually worked the second shift; he preferred it. Harris wasn't a morning person and liked to stay up late and binge watch old television shows. The second shift worked perfectly for him.

It was a pretty cool job. Easy, too.

Most days were spent swiveling back and forth in his chair

while watching the wall of monitors that spanned the office building and exterior doors.

Camera A2 was a wide-angled street view. How many times did he have to pull footage for the police because of a theft or accident?

That same camera was his window to the apocalypse. Or rather, he assumed it was the apocalypse. He didn't know, and he wasn't about to go outside and find out.

Harris had heard the news about New York about two hours before he headed in for his shift. Figuring he could watch the news at work, he went in. He was certain though to bring what he called his 'shift survival supplies.' Items such as snacks, beverages, a second lunch, and extra vape juice for his electronic cigarette, just in case things heated up and his shift relief didn't show. That had happened before. He wasn't going to take a chance of sitting there, starving, wanting badly to break into the silver supply cabinet. He made the mistake of touching that once and was written up. The one and only time he got into trouble in his six years working there.

Mr. Kobak kept valuable items in that basement in a room off the security area. Mr. Kobak was also one of those big survivalists. He'd even purchased a fifty-thousand-dollar space in one of those luxury bunkers. He planned as well for his security people. In the silver cabinet were rations, water, and other supplies for three people for ten days.

Harris couldn't recall the last time there were three people on shift.

There was also a binder with tips and guidelines for practical survival.

During the days that would come he would memorize that book, saving the other activities for later.

It seemed more like a holiday than a workday; the office was empty. Harris received a phone call from Mr. Lane stating that he wouldn't blame him if he left.

Left? Why? Why would he leave? Plus, his relief never showed up and so Harris rolled into the graveyard shift which was quite interesting on a Friday night.

The security building was a block from the cultural district. An Irish Tavern was across the street and people often parked near his building to walk to the nightlife.

That was his source of entertainment. Watching the people do the drunken strut. He was amazed at how much what was happening in New York didn't faze them.

Those same Friday night dwellers were his best indicator something was happening.

In an instant, folks went from casually walking to running, and panicked.

Harris turned on the news and they were naming cities. Cities that were hit or targeted by nuclear weapons.

He didn't hear Cleveland, so he felt safe. The people outside weren't so confident. Cars crashed outside and ten minutes before everything powered down, somehow, people were pounding on the door. How did they know about it? Were they workers in the building?

Optimistic for the best but preparing for the worst, Harris placed the locks on manual before he had no choice.

There were six people in the hall, all of them shouting, pounding.

"You're killing us!"

"Let us in!"

"Open the damn door."

Harris shook his head. He wasn't killing them. If the bombs came, *they* were the ones that were killing them. Even then, they were three stories below ground. Anything other than a direct hit, they were fine. Steel door keeping them in a room or not.

Harris wasn't letting them in. He didn't know them, and he only had rations for ten days for three people. Alone, he could make that last a long time. But alone, he'd go insane. Even though insanity wasn't very likely, Harris was consumed with guilt. He was a God-fearing Christian man, and it wasn't very Christian to let those people wait outside in a hall without any provisions.

When he last checked, four of the six remained. He didn't know where they went or why they'd even leave to go topside to the mayhem and danger.

When Harris opened the door, there were only two people left. A man and a woman. He didn't say anything to them, he just allowed them into the room, then closed and locked the door.

## White Sulphur Springs, West Virginia

When Madeline Tanner was a little girl, she had a vintage Barbie Doll Airplane. It was given to her by an aunt who got it from somewhere else. It wasn't plastic or sturdy, more so vinyl and flexible. When closed it looked neat and just like a case. When opened it was supposed to be the interior of a plane. It had a flight attendant kitchen and a seating area. The problem was, it wasn't functioning like the later airplanes. The kitchen cabinet doors were just piece soft vinyl that opened, exposing a picture.

It was the 'idea' of a plane that made it fun for her, not that she could even lift it up and pretend to fly. It was a relic of its time.

Much like the Greenbrier Mountain Bunker.

On the outside it was interesting and pretty but, on the inside, what was there wasn't altogether real or functioning.

Perhaps at one time, the bunker was state of the art.

It was partly nestled under a five-star resort and went deep under the mountain, originally designed to be the hub for congress in the event of an attack on the United States. Up to one thousand people. However, as the years progressed, and the cold war ended, the usefulness of the bunker was lessened and what was once a premier place of survival was transformed into a mockery of a time gone by, and the bunker was made into a museum.

In fact, the entire first floor was redesigned to be a casino. The other areas were roped off and made into displays. The yearly rotating of food supplies ceased.

The bunker wasn't feasible.

The soldiers had then restored it to its original purpose, and the work had started long before the attacks on American soil.

It was a safe place. Now serving as the nation's capital, the White House, and the Pentagon.

Just as Greenbrier had transformed, so did Madeline. She had gone from speaker of the house to president in less than two days.

Everything that had occurred in the previous twenty-four hours was a blur. She saw many faces, heard many names, none of which she recalled very clearly. She wasn't in the mindset to be the leader and make decisions. Not yet. She was still trying to understand what all had happened and sort out the abundance of grief she was dealing with. Grief for her friends, her family, and her country.

Her aide, Lillian, went from being helpful to being useless. Madeline understood, the shock wore off and Lillian kept repeating, "I just want to go home."

They had adjoining rooms, however the door just didn't seem thick enough for Madeline to block out the sobs that carried to her from Lillian, so she threw on some clothing and made her way to the main floor of the bunker.

It was quiet, many of the soldiers were still rearranging things, carrying boxes in and out. She slipped by them unnoticed and walked over to the far wall where, for entertainment purposes, they placed slot machines.

She had a twenty-dollar bill in the pocket of her jeans and she sat down at the Triple Seven Diamond slot machine, hitting the button slowly, hoping for a hit so she could sit mindlessly for a while until the morning arrived along with the bigger decisions.

"Ma'am." He sat down next to her. "Can't sleep?"

She paused in her playing and looked at him. His name was Troy, a Captain, Special Forces, his last name slipped her mind. She remembered him. He and his team, like her, were thrust into positions of authority and power they weren't ready to face.

"Not really, Captain. Can anyone sleep?" she asked.

"I don't know." He tilted his head. "I have a couple of my mine who are passed out pretty good. Can I offer you ..." He showed her a bottle, and in his other hand he held plastic cups. "If I am out of line, I apologize ..."

"No, not at all. Thank you. I'd love one, Captain."

"Troy." He handed her a glass. "Call me Troy."

"Then in that case." She took the drink. "Call me Madeline."

"Ma'am, I cannot do that."

"Yes … you can." She sipped it, paused, cringed at the burn, and then took another drink. "Down here, we are in this together. We are …" She closed her eyes and sounded desperate. "What are we doing here? What?"

"Aside from sitting in the corner of a bunker that was once a casino after it was a bunker, drinking really expensive bourbon and playing slots …" He shrugged. "Trying like hell to think of a way to save the country."

"Yeah, that." She sniffed. "All I keep thinking of is my husband."

"I'm sorry."

"Don't be. He's alive. I'm sure of it. Ironically, he was in this state. West Virginia. He was born here, you know?"

"No, I didn't."

"Born and bred. He likes to rent a cabin at a place called Holly River," she said. "Pretty deep in the woods. No cell service, no internet, nothing. Oh wait …" She lifted her glass then sipped. "There's a pay phone. He probably doesn't even know what happened. In fact, I am pretty sure he hasn't a clue things fell apart."

"He'll find you."

"No doubt." She held her empty glass to Troy for a refill. "In the meantime, we are a country torn asunder. Every available soldier is scattered, not to mention how many are overseas. We have rumors of a ground invasion. One already here and the big one on the way, but we can't confirm where because communications aren't reliable."

"We have farmers with pitchforks," he said.

She glanced curiously at him.

"Well, militia and citizens willing to take arms against the enemy. We're ready."

"How do we rally them?"

"We will. Just … give us a day or two."

"Hmm." She nodded. "Everything fell apart in four hours. Imagine what can happen in a day or two. Now … I'm not faulting anyone. I know everyone is trying."

"We are."

"I don't know how to try," she whispered. "This is way out of my league."

"You'll get there. We'll … get there."

"How? Why did this happen?"

"That's not important, is it?" he asked. "What is important is what we do now. And that is, take control. Take it back. This is our country, our home, and we are resilient. One way or another, and I promise you"—he splashed some whiskey in her glass—"we will take it back."

# Type 920 Hospital Ship, Pacific Ocean

She was actually Ministry of Security and not military, yet she was dressed like military: blue, gray, and white camouflage pants, combat boots, and jacket. It was the combat uniform of the People's Republic of China's Navy. Fen Shu had to dress that way, otherwise there would be a lack of respect if she stood on the deck of the ship, projecting authority in a black skirt and heels.

She was a genius with an ability to make frighteningly correct predictions for events based on calculating facts of current situations. The youngest ever to achieve such a high position of authority in security, let alone being a woman.

Fen was the heart behind the invasion of the United States. The entire take down. But all of that praise would be lost if it was found out her uncle was the president.

That was a little-known fact that she fought to keep secret.

Although, sometimes she wondered if any respect she was given was simply because of her title and job, rather than who she was.

Now she left her homeland to oversee what was being called the 'Liberate America' campaign. To some it appeared drastic but in reality, Fen's reality, the measures were needed. Insurgent movements were removed, the nuclear weapons that were deployed were a measure used not only to cripple the insurgents and imbedded terrorist but to bring pause to the country. A pause needed so Liberate America could make landfall by air and sea.

On the humanitarian front it was a campaign that would restore law and order to the territories of the United States as well as provide food, shelter, and healthcare for the citizens who had been mistreated by the government.

On the political side of the fence, it was control of commodities.

While China produced a large portion of the world's food—it produced enough to be self-sustaining—most of its output was consumed locally. And no other country in the world relied on them to eat. However, the United States was a different story. It controlled seventy percent of the world's consumable exports and control of that was invaluable.

She wanted it all. Her aspirations would push her to do all that she could to be the person who was in charge.

He or she that controlled the food ... controlled the world.

Despite the global domination prospects for her country and herself, the plan wasn't embraced by all. Many viewed it as radical, unnecessary, callous, and sneaky ... no one saw it coming, nor was there reason for it.

Unprovoked.

Words spoken by leaders such as General Jian Liu.

But Liberate America went off without a hitch and stayed under the radar before military leaders such as Liu could do anything to intervene.

His strong objections would make for an uncomfortable journey across the Pacific.

As she stood on the deck of the 920 just beyond the med staff café, she felt that uncomfortableness before she looked over her shoulder.

General Liu was an orphan who joined the army at the age of sixteen. Despite thirty years of dedicated service, he managed to have a family. A wife and two daughters. If it was even more possible, in recent years since his wife's untimely passing, Liu had thrown himself more into his work, especially with his daughters reaching adulthood.

He had no political aspiration because under his own admittance, he was too opinionated and outspoken.

Fen, who rarely feared anything, had feared him a little and she never understood why. Her job, her life, was protected, in a sense by the political power of her uncle.

Still, he spoke to her as if he didn't know her uncle was president, or he didn't care.

She peered over her shoulder as he walked her way and took a deep breath. She had successfully avoided him over the last few months, at least face to face, but now they were travelling together. Even a floating hospital the size of two football fields didn't seem quite big enough.

He cleared his throat as he approached her at the railing, his way of announcing his presence.

"General." She bowed her head in a show of respect for her elder.

He hummed, nodded in return, and faced the ocean. "While I appreciate your show of solidarity for our country and those who serve it, I believe wearing that uniform is a misrepresentation and you should consider changing it."

"I did not want the men or women who serve to see me as any different."

"You give orders that must be followed. From a different position than I. So therefore, you are different. They say if you want to be heard by the ducks you must quack like a duck. I am not sure any uniform can make you"—he glanced at her—"reach the ducks." He returned his stare back to the ocean. "If it is a matter of comfort, I am sure suitable comfortable clothing can be found."

"You speak to me with such disrespect."

"I speak to you with honesty and as an elder. As an elder, I request you not wear the uniform of the men and women who are now forced to leave their homes and families."

"They are performing their duties for a humanitarian cause," she argued.

"Save your delusions of being the next Statue of Liberty for those ignorant enough to believe that is your motivation. This …

war, and that is what it is, was short sighted in planning."

Fen roared in laughter. "Short sighted? We have successfully crippled the United States of America."

The general nodded. "By strategic nuclear hits. The high population east and west, douse a few in the middle here and there."

"And the biggest invasion ever known has made landfall."

"Yes. Yes, it has. But this is no Hollywood movie. No *Red Dawn* where we come from the sky and the Americans cower and obey."

"We have the largest army, combined with North Korea, we are preparing more soldiers than there are civilians in the United States," she argued. "Three hundred and fifty thousand are mobilized."

"Ah, yes, the biggest invasion, and another three quarters of a million waiting at sea and airfields, but in doing so, and having them ready, you have now left our homeland vulnerable. The guard dog is away."

"Vulnerable to whom?" she asked. "Who is it that you fear you cannot defeat?"

"Anyone and everyone ... combined. Not only are we about to invade and control the foremost food source of much of the world, you and your imbecilic plan have now contaminated at least thirty percent of that food supply. And when the rest of the world who rely on that food find out, the sleeping giant that awakes will be unimaginable."

Fen fumed and her face showed it. "You will not speak to me as such. I will have your position, General."

"Good," he said smugly, turning from the rail. "Take it." He then walked away.

With an angry growl, Fen smashed her fist against the railing, then reached into her pocket and pulled out a cigarette. She'd calm herself, she had to. The general was wrong. All the naysayers were and they'd all see that very shortly.

# CHAPTER TWO

## Ohio River, WV

It seemed as if the boat had stopped moving altogether. The river was still and the boat drifted center of the body of water at a painstakingly slow pace.

Perhaps if the boat was smaller. Not that it was large, but the twenty-two-foot Cuddy Cabin had some weight to it.

There were four of them in that boat, and the engine had long since died. It had sputtered to an end shortly after the four of them made their escape from a war-torn area. They were battered and beaten not only from the destruction they had witnessed for twenty-four hours straight, but from the car accident as well. An accident that occurred when they were fleeing what they believed to be foreign invaders on their land.

The four of them were wearing down.

Owen Calhoun, or Cal as everyone called him, imagined his life had he not left England. He thought of his friend, Nick, back home. How Nick was supposed to be the best man in Cal's wedding that never happened. Honeymoon to New York bought and paid for, Nick told him it was going to be a mistake to go.

*"It's gonna hurt," Nick said.*

Cal supposed Nick hadn't a clue how bad that solo honeymoon would end up hurting … physically.

As he sat on the floor of that boat, Cal rotated his arm to work the kink out of his shoulder. He watched as Jake handed Ricky his rations for the day. Jake had been a cop in New York and Ricky was a Pennsylvania store owner.

The four of them were all so different, but in the same boat physically and metaphorically.

As Jake handed Cal his rations, he seemed to freeze mid transfer.

"What is it?" Cal asked.

"That shack over there," Jake replied, then pointed. "It wasn't that far ahead of us yesterday evening. Maybe a hundred feet."

From his seat in the covered cabin area, Ricky laughed. "You're mistaken. You're saying we drifted a hundred feet in one day."

"Yeah," Jake said.

"No," Ricky argued. "We drifted more than that."

"The water is not moving … at all," Jake said sternly. "And I …" He took a moment and seemed to catch his breath. "I may be wrong."

"You alright?" Cal asked Jake.

"Yeah, yeah." Jake nodded. "Just not feeling too well."

"Me either," Ricky said. "None of us are. We're dehydrated. All of us. We're going to need to get off this boat soon."

"How?" Jake tossed his hands out. "How?"

"Blow the horn," Cal said. "Next town, we start sounding the horn."

"And what? Summon the bad guys. Shoot at us? Take us prisoner," Jake said, irritated.

"Easy." Cal lifted his hand. "We haven't seen any signs of foreign soldiers or anyone dropping from the sky in a while. No, I think we're in a good place. Just we need to alert someone. She …" He nodded his head to Louise. "Needs us to."

Louise barely moved. She sat on the floor of the boat, her body leaning against the side. She only moved to sit up and lean over the boat to vomit.

"She doesn't look good," Jake said in a whisper.

"I'm right here," Louise's voice cracked.

"Think it's her diabetes?" Jake asked.

Cal shrugged and looked down to his rations. There wasn't much water left and he offered what little he did have to Louise. She shooed his hand away. "I don't know." Frustrated, Cal ran his fingers through his hair. "I just don't …" He paused. "No, it's not her diabetes," he said with eerie confidence, staring at his hand. "It's something else." The revelation hit him the second he saw his fingers covered with his own hair. Since the bombs fell, they had been in the open and exposed. Cal didn't verbalize what it was, but he knew. The sickness, vomiting, headaches. It wasn't dehydration … it was radiation.

# CHAPTER THREE

## Cleveland, OH

The security room was their bunker, their haven. It had two rooms; one was the main security room, the other, slightly smaller, was the kitchenette. Even though it was two rooms, each hour that passed, each day, it seemed to Harris that it shrunk, and he started to second guess letting one of the strangers into the shelter.

Tobias, or Toby, or even 'The Big T' as he referred to himself, was all about five foot six and Harris would describe him as a hundred pounds soaking wet. He was no older than twenty-five, probably closer to legal drinking age, with long blonde hair that he pulled into a man bun.

Toby wasn't a bad person, probably wouldn't hurt a soul, however his ability to be unnerving was out of control.

He only seemed to bother Harris. Marissa, the thirty-something woman from accounts payable, chuckled at the young man. She even told Harris she found a distracting amusement in him.

In fact, Harris had no viable reason to get angry and want to throw him out. Yet, he felt that way quite a bit. He cherished the hours when Toby slept and dreaded when he woke up.

It was almost that time.

Harris tapped his fingers on the counter desk fast and furiously as Toby slept on a couch five feet away.

Marissa placed her hand over his to stop him. "You need to approach this differently."

"How?" asked Harris. "Tell me how?"

"You are looking at him from your position here at the firm. Security, tough guy. That's going to be fantastic when we leave here, but we're here and you aren't security. In fact, you don't project anything else."

"What do you mean?"

"You have to have a life outside this job."

"No, not really. I go home, eat, sleep, play some video games."

"You don't claim dependents, so I take it you don't have children or a spouse."

Harris just stared at her.

"Let's see ..."

"Where is this going?" he asked.

"I am trying to get you out of the security guy mind-set because I think that is the key to not getting annoyed with Toby."

"I don't think that's possible."

"You have to make it possible," Marissa told him. "We're in this together."

"No." Harris shook his head. "We are not."

"Harris, you opened the door and let us in."

"Yes. Into this room." He stood and paced. "Not into my life, not into my world. When I open this door and it's safe according to the survival manual, I'm out of here and you can deal with him."

"That doesn't make sense," she said. "Why would we separate?"

Harris shook his head. "Why would we stay together? Safety in numbers? Because Hollywood movies tell us to fraction off into groups? No. It's survival of the fittest. Look around, who do you think is the fittest? When push comes to shove, I won't have weakness pull me down." He opened the door to the kitchenette, walked inside, and closed the door.


## Swall, CA – San Joaquin Valley


A name he once painfully associated with childhood bullies became a very profitable trademark. Most people in the area or who bought his product thought 'Fat Joe' of Fat Joe's tomatoes, corn, and other vegetables was a fictitious name.

It wasn't.

Joseph Garbino had been Fat Joe for as long as he could remember. In fact, he was 'Fat Joe' long after he stopped being husky. He wasn't thin, by any means, but he was a far cry from being fat. His work was far too physical. He was a farmer and that was the only way of life he ever knew. He grew vegetables. Although he had chickens, a few horses, and a pig, they weren't for business, they were more so for his own personal needs.

He inherited the farm from his father when he was twenty-eight. By the time he was thirty, he created his own mixture of fertilizer and his tomatoes ended up being the ripest, sweetest tomatoes in the valley. When he canned them, they were a precious commodity and in high demand at flea markets and local restaurants.

Before the Fat Joe vegetable business became really lucrative, a high school friend of his drove a hundred miles to his farm one day just for his freshly canned tomatoes.

"You ought to take these tomatoes and go national," he said to Joe. "'Cause these Fat Joe tomatoes are the best around."

He had never thought about going beyond local, so when he did, just on the off chance he was successful, he named them Fat Joe's so those who picked on him in school would get a whiff of his success.

Within a few years, everyone knew him. Well, almost everyone. His distribution was still small, but mighty.

He worked so much he didn't have time for a social life. Let alone to get married. His fun was limited to cold beers on the porch with his friend and neighbor, Saul. He was also single, but due to divorce. And together, they'd hit the once-a-month bingo at the volunteer fire department.

He'd joke that he'd find that special one when he turned thirty. That didn't happen and so he moved it to forty. Then when he turned fifty and that special one never came, he said, "The hell with it." He had a nephew that he adored. He was a father figure to him when his brother, the boy's father, had died.

For the most part, Fat Joe worked. From sun up to sun down, no exceptions. Not even when the war broke out. He was motivated even more so, because people were going to be needing food.

There was no Fat Joe's factory. He had built a large barn on his property that served as a canning division.

When the bombs fell, his ten workers never showed up for work. Wouldn't make a difference, there was no power, no phones to call.

Joe worried about radiation and fallout from the bombs, so he rode over on horseback to Saul's, who owned the farm next to him.

When the Japanese Fukushima nuclear reactor melted, and the news came that radiation would arrive in California, Saul invested in the gadgets to test the air and ground. He learned them and educated himself on radiation.

Saul was younger than Joe by ten years. It wasn't that Joe was old, he wasn't, but he never bothered to learn technology the way Saul did. Following the Japanese incident, Saul checked Joe's land and gave it a clean bill.

"If mine's fine, yours is fine," Saul had said.

"Can you just check?" Joe asked.

"We're talking two nukes," Saul said. "You have to look at the wind. We're smack in between, we aren't getting anything. Plus, we're protected by the mountains."

"I don't know about that stuff," Joe said. "I have tomatoes I can pick early, I don't want them contaminated."

"They won't be. If they were, they'd be no good and you'd have to skim at least the top ten inches of your soil to grow anything."

"Can you check?"

"Fine. Fine. Let me grab Spot and I'll be right over," Saul said, referencing his horse.

Joe was grateful, and Saul did come over, run some tests and everything was good.

Still feeling uneasy, Joe worked to pull what he could, just in case.

The bombs fell on a Friday night California time, and Joe, along with everyone else, was plunged into darkness. On Sunday he went to church, prayed for those poor souls in the affected area, then picked tomatoes and beans the rest of the day. By Tuesday, it was as if nothing ever happened.

He was getting into his new routine, wake up to the rooster, wash his face, light a Sterno stove and put on the percolator to make some coffee. While that brewed he went out, checked the water and feed for the animals, came back in, poured a cup of coffee then went to the coop to get some eggs.

By the time he finished that, the lights were on. Every light in his house.

Joe rushed back in and the television was on, complete with cable.

The news was playing and he was glad about that. He and many others had been in the dark about the happenings in the world.

Mind full of questions and coffee in hand, he sat down to take in the news.

However, nothing, absolutely nothing was mentioned on the news about the bombs or the war.

He lifted the remote and switched the channel. There was some cartoon, another switch, a cooking show, another click of the remote and there was one of those morning shows. The cutesy hosts were laughing, sitting on a sofa while sipping from their coffee mugs.

Joe would have believed he dreamt the bombs or was

hallucinating, had it not been for the fact that even with cable, those four programs were all that were on.

"What the hell?"

Joe kept pressing the 'up' channel button on the remote. News, cartoon, cooking, talk show … news, cartoon, cooking, talk show …

No empty channels, no blue screen. Those four shows took up all two hundred plus channels Joe had.

Joe dropped the remote on to his chair and walked to the phone. He lifted it. There was a tone. Immediately, he called Saul.

Two rings, Saul answered.

"Hey, Saul, did I wake you?" Joe asked.

"No, not at all. I was just about to call you."

"So, I take it you noticed we have power again?" Joe asked.

"Yes, I did. It's splendid."

*Splendid?* Joe thought. *That was an odd word choice for Saul to use.* "Listen Saul, I put on the television—"

"When you should be putting on the eggs," said Saul.

"Huh?"

"I can really go for an egg, I know you have them."

"I do. But …"

"I'll be there in a jiff. Thanks for the invite."

Click.

Scratching his head, Joe stared at the phone for a few seconds. He really didn't understand anything that was going on. Everything seemed off. He did know one thing, for some strange reason, Saul was on his way over at the crack of dawn for some eggs, and Joe had better get cooking.

## Holly River, WV

Senator Gus Howard was a badass. Even though his name didn't sound it, he was. Everyone who knew him respected and feared him. A former marine, Gus ran an impressive grassroots campaign during a special election and trumped the favorite by a long shot. He was rough and rugged, showing up to events on a motorcycle, and even making no bones about his drinking and smoking pot.

As a senator he had visited war zones so much he garnished the nickname Golden Gus Cash because he always brought the troops special gifts and was constantly playing Johnny Cash.

He had made friends with Steve Tanner, husband of Speaker of the House Madeline Tanner, despite that he and Madeline were on both sides of the political aisle.

Typically, he joined Steve the entire time on those five-day fishing trips to Holly River, and encouraged them to be longer, especially after his wife passed. But on the weekend of the attack, he had an appointment for a root canal and didn't want to reschedule it. He trusted only his dentist in his hometown of Union, Pennsylvania and had returned there. It wasn't that far from the fishing site, shorter distance than Washington.

Steve left for Holly River on Thursday, the day of Gus' dentist appointment. Gus told him he'd head down Friday some time. He couldn't call him if there was trouble, that was why they picked Holly River.

There wasn't a signal for miles.

It was set so deep in the mountains that once you went into the valley, there was no contact with the outside world.

Old man Bear Grayson was a radio operator eight miles away. If there was an emergency, he got word. Plus, his phone worked because Bear was out of the valley.

Feeling better after a rough night following his root canal, Gus packed up a bag and headed for the three-hour trek to join his buddy at Holly River. He got a late start and was halfway there when all hell started to break loose, first in New York.

He thought about bypassing Holly River and heading straight to Washington like many in congress and senate were doing. After all, it was one terror attack he'd need to be there for, but he changed his mind and headed back to Union, to his home state, where his constituents were. He reached out to Bear, leaving word for him to find Steve in the morning and let him know about the attacks.

By morning though, all had changed.

The United States had not only been thrust into war, it was thrust into chaos.

Communications were down and so was most of the power.

Pittsburgh, forty miles north of him, was hit with a nuclear weapon. His small town of fifteen hundred was a ghost town.

Gus had to figure out a plan. Where was he needed? Washington was hit, that meant the president. It came so quickly, out of nowhere, no indication of war.

His next thought was to head to Holly River, get Steve, and help him find his wife.

En route to Holly River he witnessed the invasion first hand. Watched them drop from the sky. Gus knew at that second, he was no good captured or killed. He wasn't scared. He cursed them as they arrived. How dare they. It was his country.

The problem was the country was down, the military scattered, government in disarray.

They were sitting ducks.

He couldn't just sit by, no one could. He knew eventually he'd be a part of the fight to take the country back, but he couldn't do that alone. So many had invaded, a strategy was needed. He veered off the main roads to take the longer back roads to Holly River, out of sight and safe. He would use that driving time to think of a plan. Gus was good like that. As his tires spun on his journey south, so did his mind.

# CHAPTER FOUR

## White Sulphur Springs, WV

Radiation wasn't as low as Troy wanted it to be, but it had diminished enough that he told Madeline she could take a walk around the grounds, at least for a half an hour.

She needed the air. The exterior of the posh resort was so beautiful and untouched by the horrors of war, Madeline found herself in bouts of denial.

Was it real?

She, as president, was in limbo and felt as if she had to do something, but there was nothing she could do. Troy had sent out scouting teams over the previous few days and after an initial radio check, they heard nothing.

The soldiers and civilians that went out to scavenge weapons and food had returned, but those who went out directly to the areas infected by the foreign invaders were nowhere to be found.

"How many now?" Madeline asked Troy as they walked.

"There were fifty-three soldiers, we've sent out twenty to scout. We cannot send out anymore."

"We can't reclaim our country with so little."

"Chances are, the ones that invaded are taking prisoners, gathering those who can be a threat. We connected to the satellites and have some communication with the UK. Our best bet now is having them gather the troops stationed overseas. We do have a fighting chance."

"Organization is key."

Troy nodded. "Yes, it is. We need intel, we need to know where exactly they landed, where they are setting up the base of operations. All that is vital in setting up a counter attack. Unfortunately, we are now on the defensive."

"I can't do this."

"You don't really have a choice now, do you?"

As if chilled, Madeline clutched her own arms and rubbed them while shaking her head.

"We should go back in now," Troy suggested. "It's been long—"

"Captain!" a voice called from the distance.

Both Madeline and Troy turned to the sound of the voice. It came from a solider positioned on the roof.

"We have one returning," he announced. "Main drive."

Troy spun toward the tree-lined driveway.

One lone soldier made his way toward them. Troy rushed to him and Madeline followed behind.

"Captain," the soldier said, his voice tired and breath filled.

"Where are the others?" Troy asked.

"They sent me back, my team did. I had to stay off the roads," he replied. "They are firing on everyone who is armed, taking civilians. That's in Charleston and outlining areas. Seems like they're searching, too. We spoke to people traveling south, they came from Morgantown, they are saying it's all high population areas."

"This isn't a high population area," said Madeline.

Troy shook his head. "No, but we're close to D.C. and any political evacuation would be in this area. That's who they're searching for."

"Me," Madeline said.

"Probably." Troy turned back to the soldier. "How many did you see? Has to be a lot."

The soldier pursed his lips nervously before answering. "Like you said, Captain, this is a low population area. I would estimate thousands. I can't imagine what it is elsewhere."

"Oh, dear God," Madeline gasped, her hand shooting to her mouth. Her fingers trailed down across her lips and she glanced up to Troy. "What was that you were saying about having a fighting chance?"

## The Kremlin, Russia

He sat.

In a slight lean, legs crossed, the president sat before his office window staring out. He had been that way for a while, just staring. Watching what he could as time passed quickly. His intelligence was all over the place.

When news reached him about the first round of attacks on the United States, he was told it was homegrown domestic terrorists. A movement named Free America that would cause not only disruption but the takeover of the government. He himself had dealt with such rebels before. The almighty and righteous United States of America was finally experiencing what other countries had experienced. The United States preached, and possibly the rebels were always there, but never did they cause such an uproar.

The arrival of that news brought a sense of 'I told you so' and the president refrained from calling the leader of the United States.

Let them work it out.

Then the bombs fell.

*They're nuking their own soil?* The thought bewildered the president, it was drastic.

Still … let them work it out. Allow the dust to settle and spearhead a humanitarian effort. He couldn't imagine the chaos the United States would be under. After all, three cities were hit during 911 and it brought the US to a grinding halt. He could only imagine what ten nuclear warheads would do.

Then more intelligence poured in.

They came from submarines. Some were intercepted. Fingers were pointed at Russia and he denied responsibility.

Finally, the news of those responsible was startling. Without provocation The People's Republic of China declared war on the United States. Their sneak attack came simultaneously and under the guise of the Rebel initiative. Even giving their campaign a similar name: Liberate America.

The Russian president needed to know what was going on. It was a matter of world safety.

The problem was, China went dark. They didn't deny or boast. No news came from China, no chatter, even the internet was down. Deliberately, they had been taken back to the stone age.

The attack on the United States, the silence of China … not only was there chaos in the States, it was spreading like wildfire, like a disease with no cure.

At least three days after the bombs, the veil was lifted. Not only did China go back online, all of their news outlets were reporting the massive victory and how the people in the United States were cheering in the streets.

It didn't make sense. None of it. They crippled the United States with diversions of nuclear weapons on mainly populated areas, then during the radio blackout, they invaded.

Now, news of unrest in his own country came to his desk and as he stared out the window, the Russian president, with a heavy heart, had some tough decisions to make.

He would take his time in choosing what course of action he would or would not take.

The cost was too steep if he made the wrong decision.

# CHAPTER FIVE

## Office of the Prime Minister, England

Prime Minister Adriene Winslet was once likened by the press to Margaret Thatcher. It was an American media station and she took it with a grain of salt. Americans always likened every British female politician to Thatcher, just like those in the UK likened every conservative American president to Ronald Reagan.

Winslet wasn't as staunch or iron clad on things like Thatcher was. In fact, more times than not, she was pretty passive, and wished at this moment in time she could channel Margaret Thatcher because the situation needed it.

It boiled down to the good of an ally or the good of the country, because under the current situation, it posed more of a threat to help the United States than it did a benefit.

In fact, her own country was in turmoil, much as every other industrialized nation.

The stock markets crashed, and it had been a week since any

imports arrived from overseas.

There was no word on that.

Shops, despite warning from the government, were price gouging as shelves increasingly grew empty. Half the population cried out for the government to do something—*feed your people*—while the other half sought violence.

Riots were an everyday occurrence and the military had been deployed to the streets with a strict, sun up to sun down ordinance.

It wasn't working. The workforce for essential services was running about forty percent; people just didn't go to work. Mass transportation had come to a halt, and within a week of the American bombings, nine terrorist attacks within London claimed a thousand lives.

Everything was falling apart.

She had citizens in the United States and hadn't heard from any of them. Winslet was within her right to go and retrieve her people but she, like many other leaders, didn't have a clue what was happening there.

The last the People's Republic of China said was to defend their presence as humanitarian. They declined any further comment and balked at the threats made to them by Russia.

If indeed China had settled in America and claimed it, they controlled a good portion of the world's food supply.

They'd have the upper hand. No amount of threats was going

to make a dent, not when the world needed that food.

The only positive to it all was there had not been word of a surrender. Though that didn't mean much. Winslet hadn't heard from the president in days. That frightened her because the president wasn't elected as leader, she was in a sense drafted because of her position in congress.

Before it all, Winslet never liked her, thought she had a big mouth, was always in the news for spouting off. But when things went down, Winslet believed that the president's 'big mouth' would be an asset.

Suddenly the mouthy woman grew quiet and timid.

Who was Winslet kidding, every leader in the world had.

They just didn't know what to do.

Perhaps collectively as leaders a solution could be devised. Winslet prepared for the emergency summit called by Russia.

Hopefully, heads together, something would be done.

Should they? Should anyone get involved?

Any confrontation could, and more than likely *would*, cause global catastrophe

The bottom line was Winslet didn't have to get involved in order for her country to be destroyed. She watched it unfold out of her Downing Street window. It was going to happen either way. It was just a matter of picking the path of least destruction.

# Type 920 Hospital Ship, Pacific Ocean

There were six of them in that conference room all sitting around the table, all military leaders, and General Liu was one of them. They sat in silence, none of them speaking. The general knew what that was; there was a level of trust that was missing, and no one wanted to say anything for fear of repercussion. Hours from making landfall, they were brought together for the same purpose: to be informed of the mission and what would happen next.

General Liu knew what they were waiting for, or rather who. On the table were two pitchers of water and glasses, and before each of them was a folder with a region number on it. The United States had been divided into six different regions, similar to the nine that FEMA had. General Liu hadn't opened his folder yet to look at the map. Because of his negative interactions with Fen, he was rather certain his region would be that of the north east. An area where cities like Boston, New York, Pittsburgh, Philadelphia, and Washington D.C. were. He figured he would be given the virtual wasteland.

The number four was large on the front of his folder and he opened it to look. He was surprised to see that his area was in the state of Texas, and included portions of a few of the surrounding states. The one area of the United States where only a single nuclear weapon had fallen. The population in that area was dense. After thinking about it, it made sense. General Liu was more a man of the people and related well to the population.

The door opened, and all six men around the conference table stood when Fen walked in the room. She wasn't alone like on the deck; she was accompanied by two armed guards dressed in suits. Probably an intimidation tactic. General Liu noticed that she'd taken his advice and dressed differently. She wore a fitted skirt and white blouse, with her hair pulled tightly back into a bun as she presented a stern expression.

"Please be seated," she said. "Ten nuclear weapons were successfully detonated over American soil. There were more but they had been intercepted. The weapons were detonated over military and densely populated areas and strategically placed to cause chaos. We, gentlemen, will be there to pick up the scattered and the lost. The first two phases of the plan have finished. At least one city in each of your areas was affected by the bombs. Part of the mission now is to go in, aid the sick and injured, bury the dead, and help those who are displaced. Gain trust with community leaders and be a presence. A strong presence. We take prisoners of those who are resistant and violent. All US soldiers in uniform are to be imprisoned within the affected areas. Once the radiation in those areas has reached a safe level, the process of cleaning will commence."

Another general raised his hand. "So, I am to assume we have received a surrender?"

"No." She shook her head. "We are currently still looking for the individual serving as president."

"Do we know who they are and if there is one?"

"We are following intel regarding access to classified communications systems. We have not blocked that for this reason. So we can track the acting president."

"You haven't found him. Then why are we moving this deeply into planning?" he asked. "Without a surrender there's a possibility that this war will continue. That it is not over."

"It's just a matter of time. A very short period of time," she said. "The surrender is coming. Confidence is high. How can it not?" She then paused to look around the table before continuing. "I have spoken of the areas of destruction. There are three hundred million people in the United States of America. We estimate current casualties are in excess of eight million. Estimated injuries are in the tens of millions. The majority of the country and their countrymen are still standing and physically unaffected. And we now enter into what I like to call the complacent phase."

*And that is?* General Liu thought.

Fen continued, "Right now, in various areas of the country, the infrastructure is healing. Phone and cell service has been restored, limited, restricted, and monitored internet, comparable to our own, access to banks and credit and of course, the television. Although we control what they see, they have been given a sense of normalcy. When Americans do not hear the news twenty-four-seven, they forget. They are easily satisfied when they are complacent. It may seem silly, but keep them occupied, distracted, and at some level of normalcy and they will fall in line."

"So, what you are saying …" General Liu said. "If an uprising or rebellion begins, we are hoping that those who are complacent will say, it's better having this than none."

"In a sense." Fen nodded. "But there is more to this. We need to make them want us there through need. Welcome us. Be grateful for our presence."

It wasn't supposed to happen, but General Liu stifled a laugh. It came out more like a cough.

"Problem?" Fen asked.

Liu took a deep breath, tapping his hand on the folder. "We invaded their country …"

"They don't know that."

"What?"

"Not all. Most are under the impression that domestic terrorists did this. That was the last news most people heard. Our presence could be taken as our attempt to control."

"Don't be too sure of that," General Liu said.

"I'm not, but I am sure of the next part of my plan. The part that will make them need us and be grateful we are here."

"And that is?" General Liu asked.

Presenting a smug expression, Fen then pressed her lips

together in a brief closed-mouth smile. "You'll find out very shortly."

## Ohio River, Hanlen, WV

The scent of the river carried up to Cal's nose and hit him hard, the odor was all consuming. It reeked of garbage and fish, and it took everything Cal had not to vomit into the water. He didn't know, though, if the river was really that bad or if his current heightened sense of smell was making it seem that way.

Out of the four of them, Cal was doing the best, but none of them were really well. He supposed had they not run out of water, they'd be better.

Dehydration had set in.

Louise had taken the last of her insulin and was so weak and lethargic, Cal doubted she'd make it through the day.

When the realization hit them that they were experiencing radiation sickness, they were angry.

*What were they thinking?*

That thought was verbalized amongst them all.

"We should have known," Jake said. "I'm pissed because we should have known. It was a nuclear bomb, of course there'd be radiation. We should have known to find shelter, at least the first day or two."

"We did have shelter," Ricky added. "My store. But we were so concerned with leaving, going away from the bombs, we didn't think." He looked at Cal. "Your poor girlfriend, man."

Cal reached over and gently ran his hand down Louise's back. It wasn't that they were a couple, they had potential to be, they started to be, then everything went to hell.

Louise was a bright spot during a really dark time for Cal. She brought a spark of life back to him when he felt dead inside. He wanted badly to give her that feeling, life, spark, hope … but he couldn't, nothing could.

She was really sick. She not only clung to the side of the boat, she clung to her life.

They were all at a loss as they floated in what would be an open coffin down the wide Ohio River.

A cruise of death.

Stalled in the middle and none of them had the strength to swim ashore.

It was ironic. When Cal and his almost-wife planned the honeymoon, a cruise was an option. If they had gone with that, Cal would have been on the non-refundable cruise instead of in America when the bombs fell.

He would have been alive, fine, afloat on the ocean, sipping margaritas while listening to the news about world. Shaking his head, proclaiming his sorrow over the events, all while having all of his hair.

He had lost a few patches, although he probably wasn't as bald as he felt. The scars and cuts on his hands from the accident had turned into blistering sores.

Everyone on the boat experienced that. If they had an open cut, it became an unsightly seeping wound.

He was able to sleep a little the night before, but knew things were bad when he woke up. His mouth was so dry his tongue felt like sandpaper to the roof of his mouth. To top it all off, he'd started to hallucinate.

Across the river, on the shore, he thought he saw the Morton Salt Girl. Dressed in all yellow, she stood on a pier staring out. Then she multiplied, there were three more of her, giving new meaning to double vision.

Cal watched as the Morton Salt Girl and her trail of clones climbed in a boat.

*It's not real*, Cal thought. There was no reason for the Morton Salt Girl to be on the river's edge.

In his weakness he rested his head on the side of the boat and his hand on Louise's back. He closed his eyes and started to drift into sleep until he heard the sound of a motor.

He wanted to lift his head, but he lacked the strength, even moving it slightly caused everything to spin.

The motor sound drew nearer and then it cut off and was

replaced with voices.

"I knew I saw people," a woman said.

"The question is, are they alive?" a man asked.

"That one is," another man answered. "How about those two?"

Cal parted his lips to call out and opened his eyes slightly. Immediately, a bright light nearly blinded him.

"He is. They all are. Barely."

They continued to talk, and the boat moved a little, rocking back and forth. Cal wasn't sure if it was real or if it was a sleep deprived, dehydration hallucination. If it was a hallucination it was vivid. Cal's sense of smell kicked in again, and he could smell rubber and cigarettes.

"Should we transfer?" a man asked.

"No," the woman answered. "We'll tow them to shore. I'll ride with them while you hitch it. Radio Doc and tell him we have four nor'scapes on the way in."

"You really think they're nor'scapers?" asked a man.

"Yeah, I do," she replied. "They all got exposure sickness. The woman is bad. They're adrift in a stalled boat. So, yeah, they ran from the north."

"All hitched," someone announced, then the boat jolted as the motor rumbling sounded again.

The boat began to move slowly, and Cal lifted his head.

"No, no," she said to him. "Rest. We'll be there shortly. We'll get you some help. No worries."

No worries?

Cal was nothing *but* worries.

He did as suggested and rested his head down again.

He hoped the second boat, the four Morton Salt People, were real and not some elaborate dream. Because being real meant rescue, hope, and a not-so-imminent death sentence.


## Cleveland, OH


Every single bit of their supplies was spread out on the counter top desk in the main security room of the basement bunker.

Harris manned the supplies, separating them into piles, while he nibbled on his afternoon ration for the day. He tried to stay focused on that task, even contemplating going in the other room to do it because Toby sat on the floor, doing his Toby thing … talking.

Marissa didn't help matters much. When she wasn't smiling over things he said, she was asking him questions like a talk show host.

"That's when I took the Mega Bus," Toby said. "I could have

flown. But like, everyone was talking about this Mega Bus on the east. So I had to try it. I mean, after all, I was on the east, right? Was headed to Cleveland."

"From Atlanta?" Marissa asked.

Toby nodded. "One problem though."

Harris mumbled. "Mega Bus doesn't stop in Cleveland."

"Dude!" Toby shouted with excitement. "Yes. You're right. No one told me. I ended up in Indianapolis. I thought something was up when we totally missed Ohio."

"You think maybe you should have checked first?" Harris asked.

"No. I wasn't in a hurry. I took another bus here. It wasn't as nice though."

"What brings you to Cleveland?" Marissa asked.

"Rock and Roll Hall of Fame." Toby held a slender tan pouch, about an inch wide and four inches long. He squeezed the last remnants of its peanut butter contents in his mouth. "So good. You know why peanut butter is in survival stuff, right?"

Marissa shook her head.

"It's an appetite suppressant. Put a little peanut butter in ya, you don't want to eat as much. That's how I lost two hundred pounds."

Harris immediately stopped what he was doing. "Wait. What? Two hundred pounds. No way."

"Dude. Right hand to God." Toby raised his hand. "I was huge. Lost a hundred and eighty-two and when they cut the extra skin off, I dropped another twenty or something like that."

"From eating peanut butter?" Marissa asked.

"Not just peanut butter. When my dad died, I got depressed and my weight like maxed out. My uncle took me in. You might know him, he's pretty B-level famous in the west. Fat Joe."

"Of Fat Joe's tomatoes?" Marissa said excitedly. "I love Fat Joe's tomatoes."

"How did a guy called Fat Joe get you to lose weight?" Harris asked.

"First, he's not fat anymore," Toby told him. "Second, he said to me, 'Tobias, you fat fuck ...' Okay maybe not those words, but he thought it. He told me, 'You'll work and eat right and limit the video games.' And bam, I lost the weight pretty much over a summer. Maybe into fall."

"Just by eating peanut butter," Harris said in disbelief.

"Dude, no, weren't you listening? Peanut butter was part of it. He used to make me eat a teaspoon before each meal. Then I had to eat two slices of tomatoes, any style, a glass of water and then I could have whatever I wanted. By then, I wasn't hungry. Plus, I was out of school and he worked my butt off. I'm like an ace farmer now. Total asset in an apocalypse world. Dude, do you know how many calories you burn milking a cow?"

"No." Harris shook his head. "How many?"

Toby shrugged. "I don't know. I thought maybe you did."

"Jesus," Harris said with irritation. "I have to get back to this. So, we all have our stuff when we leave."

"Since you're being anti, you could put mine and M's stuff in one pile. We're traveling together."

"And where are you two going?" Harris asked.

"Indiana, her family," Toby answered. "She said it's farmland."

"No," Marissa corrected. "The name of the town is Farmland."

"Cool."

"And you're going to walk?" Harris asked.

"If we have to. I'm gonna look for a bus and jump it." Toby nodded. "Where are you going?"

"I live about five miles south of here, I'm gonna see if my house is alright."

"You're saying we're leaving in a couple days, right?" Marissa asked. "Are we sure? I mean I want to get out of here as much as you do but are we sure?"

"Yeah," Harris answered. "The book says so."

"But in movies, radiation lasts for decades. Areas are deadly for centuries."

"Not so," Toby said. "Radiation has a half-life. Gotta follow the seven ten rule."

"The seven ten rule?" Marissa questioned.

"Yeah it's how the radiation falls tenfold every seven hours."

Harris scoffed in a laugh. "Please, how do you know this?"

"Dude, just because I'm a pothead doesn't make me dumb. Speaking of which, man I can't wait to get out of here and smoke."

"Smoke?" Harris said sarcastically. "I take it you mean the marijuana. How exactly do you plan on getting it? I'm pretty sure your dealer has other things to worry about."

"Dude, simply because you called it, 'the marijuana' tells me you don't know too many potheads. I have it. In my backpack. I would have already fired up but you two are so straight, I figured you'd get pissed if I did that in this closed in space."

"You have marijuana in your backpack? How much?"

"Enough." Toby shrugged.

Harris held out his hand. "Let me see."

"You aren't gonna try to play security dude and confiscate my illegal stash, are you?"

"No, I want you to get it, so we can all smoke a little and relax."

"Dude, sweet." Toby got up and went into the other room.

"You know," Marissa said, "it makes you hungry and thirsty."

"We'll dip. I'm not worried about finding rations after we get out of the city."

"Really?"

"Really. Yeah, some cities got hit by terrorists. We're a big country. Right now, everyone is rallying, looking for survivors."

"You don't think this is more than terrorists?"

Harris shook his head. "I do not. I think once we make our way out, we're gonna be surprised how fine everything really is," he said. "I believe it."

## Swall, CA – San Joaquin Valley

"Well, when you said you wanted eggs," Joe said to Saul in the kitchen, "I didn't think you wanted me to be your own personal Waffle House."

"You have the best eggs in the county."

"Yeah, well you could have made them yourself." Joe set the plate of two fried eggs in front of Saul.

"Look at these, perfect." Saul grabbed his fork. 'Say, have you heard from Toby?"

Gripping the back of a chair, Joe shook his head. "No. But that kid is smart. I don't believe for one second he got caught up in trouble. He's safe, I feel it."

"That's good."

"Listen, you got me confused, I called you to talk about …"

"Eggs."

"Goddamn it, Saul. Listen …"

"Let's go outside." Saul stood.

"What about your eggs?"

Saul grabbed the plate and walked out the kitchen door.

It took a second delay, but Joe followed. By the time he made it outside, Saul was standing a good distance from the house eating his eggs.

Clearly, his friend had lost his mind.

Joe took the gentle approach and cautiously walked to Saul. "What's happening, my friend?"

"I didn't want to be in the house in case it was bugged."

"What do you mean bugs?"

"Not bugs as in buzz-buzz insects. Bugs as in listening devices."

"Oh, now …" Joe waved out his hand.

"Oh, now, what? No. No. That's why I came over. I don't trust the phones."

"The television is awfully screwy. It's like the twilight zone. People are all happy and chipper and not one word about the bombs."

"Exactly. It's like none of it happened. But it did. That's why I don't want to talk on the phone."

"Why would they listen?" Joe asked.

"Because they need to hear what's going on," Saul said. "They need to hear if people are planning a rebellion."

"Hold on." Joe lifted his hand. "I watched the news when things started. This was all some terrorist group made up of Americans. Very un-American but Americans nonetheless."

"I think it's more," Saul said. "The un-Americans had help. They had to. There is no way they got the power up, the phones, and the televisions. Not on this level. I heard ... I heard there were soldiers from another country parachuting from the sky."

"Like that movie?"

Saul nodded.

"What country?" Joe asked.

"I don't know. A big one. Like I said has to be big to get things up and running so fast."

"Why would they do that?" Joe asked. "If they are gonna invade our country why would they make us comfortable?"

"That's easy," Saul said. "We're comfortable. We don't fight back." He took a huge hunk of eggs and placed it in his mouth.

"Honestly, Saul, even if the kitchen was bugged or the phones. Nothing we said here can be taken wrong. We aren't rebels."

"Not yet."

Joe looked quickly at him. "What are you saying? Take arms and fight?"

"War and fighting is a young man's game. Survival is a farmer's game. That's how we fight. Right now, you and I have to find a way to get our crops and food and hide it. Hide it somewhere fast. Before this other country takes control of the farm."

"Will they do that?" Joe asked.

"I would. Control the food, control the people."

"Starve the fighters."

Saul nodded. "So, you and I have to control what we can now. Stock it. Store it. Hide it. We can do our part in this rebellion by being a safe place for food, supplies, and to hide."

"You think they'll be a rebellion?" Joe asked.

"Oh, without a doubt. This is America. We're gonna fight back. We're gonna help."

"I'm in, man, but the television, you wouldn't even know anything was wrong."

"That's exactly how they want it. After a while people will believe it," Saul said. "And that's what makes this all even more scary."

## Holly River, WV

Steve Tanner worried about his wife, but Bear Grayson told him to "pipe down" about it. Last he heard through radio chatter she was safe and sound in a government bunker.

Then Bear followed it with, "However, if I am picking up that chatter, the enemy is too."

Bear was a no-nonsense, old war vet who had lived on the mountain for fifty years. He was a communications specialist in the war and conveyed to Steve that no means of communications were safe.

"How the hell are we supposed to gather forces?" Steve asked.

"What are you shooting for?" Bear asked.

"Right now, our men and women of the military are out there. You know they want to fight. You know that people like me, you, they want to fight. We need to organize."

"Yes, we do, but we can't go halfcocked, get a bunch of goofs together and attack a brigade. We need a strategy. We need intel. Ten men with a plan can do a lot more damage than a hundred running haywire."

"But if they hear what we're saying, how do we reach out?" Steve asked.

"It's less a matter of them hearing and more of them understanding."

"What do you mean?"

"I mean. I can get on the radio and say, 'hey all you guys ready to be part of the resistance, tomorrow fluff Barney the Dinosaur's tail.'"

"What the hell does that mean?"

"Exactly."

"It means ..." Gus' voice entered the room. "Code words. Code phrases. They can listen all they want, but if they are clueless to what we're saying, we have the upper hand."

Bear looked at Gus. "Don't you knock?"

"You're on the sun porch, Bear, the door was open."

"Oh, yeah, that's right, trying to air it out from Stevie Boy here. He ain't smelling that good."

Steve facially grimaced at him, then walked to Gus and embraced him. "Glad you're here."

"Safest place I know," Gus said. "I don't expect it to be long before others join us. We can get and secure the east coast, then hit others using Bear's coded methods. I've been spreading the word from home to here. Letting them know this is home base. Word will travel."

Bear looked at him curiously. "Word will also travel to the enemy."

"Eh," Gus waved out his hands. "I don't expect the Procs to even get this."

"Procs?" Steve asked.

"People's Republic of China," Gus answered.

"Hot damn." Bear smacked his hand on the desk. "That is a good one. Lot easier than saying People's Republic of China, that's for goddamn sure."

"How are you spreading the word?" Steve asked.

Gus reached to his back pocket and then set down a bright orange flyer. On it was a big fish center and the words:

*Gene Autry Fishing Battle*

*Hosted by Gus Cash*

*Holly River, WV*

*Refreshments provided by Honeymoon Chinese*

"There you have it," Bear said. "Any soldier knows Gene Autry. That's a call out to warriors. Gus here, his name is famous, they see that they know he is organizing. The Chinese food is a nice touch to say it's against the Chinese."

"You posted these?" Steve asked.

"Everywhere I could," Gus said.

"They're good. But honestly, Gus, just my opinion," Steve said. "With all that's going on, I don't think a single person is going to understand your coding. So don't feel bad if no one shows up."

# CHAPTER SIX

## Eight Days Later – Ten Days Post Bombs

## White Sulphur Springs, WV

Everything was technologically old. Despite the bunker being up-dated and refitted in parts, the communications room of Green-brier had not been touched in decades. The computer system looked like an advertisement from the RadioShack Tandy computer days. Black screen, green lettering, blinking block of light. But they worked. They did their job.

Troy had brought with him an emergency communications computer system. Locked in that lead case, which also served as a faraday cage. The program looked like those in the communica-tion room, an old DOS operating system.

It took several days for them to get a steady connection to communication. It was hit and miss. Up and down. They'd con-nect to the satellite, and just as they would to get an image, the satellites would go down. Finally, through a secure and hidden area of the internet, Troy connected them to the UK. From there, the techno geniuses of Great Britain worked to get them together and online. Finally, there was talk.

"We have a bit of trouble here. Unrest. Concerns," said Prime Minister Winslet. Her voice stayed cool and calm. Never wavering. "We pick up bits and pieces of radio from your side. Not much. Just seems everything is blocked. We're working on it."

"I know you are," said Madeline. "I appreciate it."

"How are you holding on?" asked the prime minister.

"I feel like a mouse in a maze."

"Understandable."

"So, you've not been drawn in?" Madeline asked.

"Not yet. The population of Great Britain is in turmoil over what to do. However, I have received word from Russia. We're meeting for the summit in two days."

"The summit?"

"Yes," the prime minister said. "The Russian president has called several countries together. So we collectively can figure out what course of action we are going to take whether it be held or otherwise."

"I take it China want to be there?"

There was no response.

"Prime Minister?"

"China is denying all culpability in this. Flat out denying it."

"What?" Madeline said with almost a laugh. "They're here. Reports that I'm getting show they're here in masses. Military presence."

"Yes. But they claim they are there as goodwill ambassadors and also for humanitarian reasons."

"That's bullshit."

"You know that, and I know that," the prime minister said. "I'm pretty certain the world knows it as well. But no one can make a move without knowing one hundred percent what the situation is over there."

"Unfortunately, I can't ..." Madeline paused to cough. "I can't fill you in ... because ..." She coughed again. "I have no idea where normal clothes are let alone ..." Again, she coughed. A dry hacking cough.

"Are you alright?"

"I think ..."

"Shit," Troy blurted out.

"What?" Madeline asked.

"Smoke." He pointed to the vent.

Madeline peered up to the thin white stream of smoke that poured in. "Prime Minister, I have to call you back. We have a problem here."

"Absolutely."

Madeline disconnected the call and stood.

"Sam," Troy called another soldier in the room. "Escort the president out until we can find out the source of the smoke."

"Right away, sir." He placed a hand on Madeline's back. "This way, ma'am."

Madeline didn't know what to expect when she left the communications room. Would the halls and main areas be filled with smoke, was the fire nearby? She was confused because not a single alarm went off. But as she grew farther away from the communications room, there wasn't any smoke.

Sam led her with urgency toward the former casino area and to the huge steel door.

"Sam? What's going on?" a soldier asked. "Everything okay?"

"Captain is looking for the source of smoke," Sam replied. "Get some guys together and see if he needs help?"

"What smoke?"

"It's in the back." Sam pulled the door opened with a grunt, enough for them to slip out, then he secured the door again.

The passageway to the top was a long, sloped tunnel lit by sporadic emergency lights. It was an exhausting ordeal to walk it and Madeline's legs ached and she began to get winded from the pace.

Finally, she felt a renewed sense of stamina when she saw the sun from the open doors. It was unusual because they were never left open. She figured someone got the word about the smoke and opened them.

Even though it was overcast, it was still bright, and Madeline's eyes started to adjust before she stepped out.

Once outside, the temporary blindness was replaced with shock. She froze and didn't move. In fact, she did the only thing she could think of and that was to raise her hands.

It was the only thing she could do.

At the west entrance of the bunker, seemingly waiting for her, was a line of at least forty foreign soldiers all aiming their weapons at her.


## Air China, Flight to San Antonio, Texas

Not including the two flight attendants and pilots, General Liu was one of only two people aboard the large aircraft. It had been restructured long before the invasion to include a flying meeting room, designed to accommodate an entire government team in the air with its plush, wide chairs that were set up in rows of four, face to face, like a train car. There was a conference table and small bar. But the general sat alone. His finger ran over the rim of his glass that contained his slightly warmed baijiu. He sipped it occasionally while staring out of the window. His computer tablet was on the small table before him. He would get to that. He just needed to think. Across from him were two empty seats, in fact all around were empty seats.

It was a waste of fuel, he didn't need to ride in comfort. Plus, waiting for his day to board the plane put him days behind schedule. He could have been in Texas for days already.

San Antonio was a large city with one point four million people. It was two hundred miles west of Houston Ground Zero. The entire state was going to be a challenge to him. The more he looked at what he had to oversee, the more he realized he had the biggest problem area. The biggest headache was the fact that Fen would set up her headquarters there as well.

The entire military campaign was absurd and obviously masterminded by someone without decades of experience. It wasn't thought through; while they would claim it was, Liu knew better.

He likened it to the many times he chuckled when America's CIA initiated something under the guise of a military action. Always it failed.

Ms. Shu and her team had been following the chatter about the domestic terrorist disruption and attempt to take and overthrow the US government. They inserted themselves into it, having moles inside so they could swiftly take over, manipulate, and control it, claiming the largest 'land invasion' in history.

Soldiers of the People's Republic of China put their lives on the line. Monetarily, it was going to be a nightmare. Moving ships, aircraft, and humanitarian aid.

Sending food to a country in chaos from a country that produced only enough to feed themselves. The only 'smart' part of Shu's plan was to get the nonaffected areas up and running as if nothing was wrong. Put the country back to work. Even then, Liu wasn't sure that would work.

Four years earlier while at a training exercise, Liu was asked how he would invade and take over the United States if need be.

He had a simple solution.

Buy them.

Buy every single debt of the United States then claim ownership.

He was laughed at. He wondered now how many of his comrades were laughing as their sons went to war.

Liu's attention was disrupted for a moment, when the flight attendant quietly placed his lunch on the table. He nodded a thank you to her and she left. A few seconds later, Fen sat across from him and was given her lunch.

"Thank you," she said to the flight attendant.

"An entire plane," said the general. "Yet you choose to sit with me."

"You've been quiet and we have much to discuss."

"I have been quiet because I am thinking about the one

hundred and seventy-three thousand military that are in Texas, and the report that we have not secured nine of the fifteen bases. Nine? How have we not secured that many?"

"It is concerning, yes." She nodded. "But we have now secured something better."

"And that is?"

With an arrogant smile she lifted her drink to her lips. "The new President of the United States."

# CHAPTER SEVEN

## Hanlen, WV

There was a point when Cal lost consciousness. Sometime between the arrival of the yellow suit people and his journey, full speed, on his back down a hallway. The overhead lights seemed to have a strobe effect, causing even more confusion on his part.

"Sir, sir," a male voice called to him. "What is your name?"

Cal's head went side to side. It was hard to tell what exactly ailed him, he felt so poorly.

"Sir, do you hear me? Look at me."

Cal blinked, the light above the man's head made him a shadow. He could only make out a little of his face, and even that was blurry.

"What is your name?"

"Cal. Owen Calhoun."

"Owen, listen to me, I need you to stay with me. Try to stay awake. Okay?"

"Cal, my name ..." he groaned, his head going side to side trying to see what was going on. One minute he was lucid the next he was grappling with reality and a plethora of noises he couldn't discern. Moans, talking, shouting.

"Mr. Calhoun, do you know the names of the people you were with?" he asked, grabbing Cal's arm.

Cal felt a pinch. "Um ... Louise."

"The woman's name is Louise."

"Diabetic."

"She's diabetic? Thank you. The two men? Their names?"

"Rick. Ricky. The cop ... Jake."

"Thank you. Do you ..."

Cal jolted when he heard a painful cry, a woman, it was close. Out of breath and panicked, Cal tried to get up. "Louise. That was Louise."

"Calm down."

"Where am I? Who are you?" Cal felt the sudden sensation of warmth running through his veins. "Where?"

"You're at an expedient medical station." The man's voice sounded distant, echoing, and it began to fade. "Mr. Calhoun, stay with us."

What was happening? Why did things start to spin ... float...?

"Mr. Calhoun?"

A long beep rang out.

Everything went black.

Gasp!

Cal jolted and his eyes opened wide as he wheezed, loudly at first. He thought he'd just dozed off, a brief instant of passing out, then he realized it was more than that. It was quiet, the multitudes of voices and the mayhem were gone.

He tried to move but as soon as he did, his entire body hurt. His chest especially. He cringed and reached for his chest when he realized he was hooked to monitors. He tilted his head to the left to try and see what was going on. The overhead lights were bright and everything farther than a few feet away was blurry.

"Wonderful," a gentle female voice said. "You're awake."

Cal looked up to the woman leaning over him. She smiled with a gentleness, a few strands of blonde hair dangled in her face as she glanced down. The rest of her hair was pulled back.

"Don't try to move. You're hooked up. I need to get a doctor."

"How long was I passed out?"

"Passed out? No." She forced a closed mouth smile. "Unconscious, coma. You've been in critical condition."

"How long?"

"I don't know for sure. I just was transferred here yesterday. I believe five days."

"Five days?" Cal groaned. "How was I critical? Was it the radiation sickness?"

"You suffered a cardiac arrest."

"I had a heart attack?"

She nodded. "It did allow your body to rest enough that we could treat the radiation. You are recovering. The road ahead is long for you. I won't lie."

"Who are you?" Cal asked.

"Leana. I'm a nurse here," she answered.

"The people … the people I came in with. Where are they?" Cal asked.

She shook her head. "I don't know. Who did you come in with? I can check."

"Please. I need to know if they're okay. Especially the woman. They came with me. Jake, Ricky, and Louise."

"Any last names?"

Cal closed his eyes. "I'm drawing a blank."

"That's fine." She placed her hand on his. "I'll go see what I can find out. I'll be back. In the meantime, please don't move."

Cal nodded as his form of agreement. Leana slipped her hand from his and walked away. Cal blinked several times, clearing the blurriness form his eyes. He was in some sort of large room, a gymnasium perhaps. Even though things were still a bit visually foggy, Cal could still see he wasn't alone in that gym, far from it. All around him were people, massive amounts of people, all laying on cots in a pseudo hospital setting. Upon seeing that, he rested his eyes again. Clearly it was going to take Nurse Leana a while, and what else did he have to do but lie there.

## Cleveland, OH

Toby's assessment about the building had been correct. He theorized that it was still standing, or at the very least it hadn't collapsed, blocking them in. He came to this conclusion because people left. When Harris didn't let them in, those who lacked patience abandoned the basement hallway. They took the stairs and never returned. Either they made it out or were somehow killed.

Toby was banking on the former.

They had no idea what was waiting for them when they left the bunker. They stayed on the assumption that the bombs were nuclear. They had been so cut off that anything was possible when they emerged.

For all they knew everything could be gone, or they'd step outside to rescue workers and a media circus.

No matter how much he tried to mentally prepare for the

worst, there wasn't enough mental preparation in the world for Toby.

His heart shattered, and Cleveland wasn't even his hometown.

They carried the remaining provision with them and slowly ascended the stairs.

Three flights up steps. That was all they had to endure.

The second they hit the first set of stairs, the smell of old smoke permeated the air. The second staircase brought blackened walls and charred debris scattered about. Just as they hit street level, they had to climb over chunks of concrete and wood.

The door was warped but it opened enough for them to slip through.

Before the attack, the stairwell opened into a wide, long hallway with swirling gray marble floors. The hallway wasn't far from the main foyer.

It was hard to even discern a floor, there was so much rubble around them. Like walking a maze, they navigated around the fallen beams and mounds of destruction. While the building was technically still standing, it had become a mere skeleton of what it was.

Their journey from the basement to the outside was a quiet one.

It was daylight, but the sky was heavily overcast, and

everything had a gray feel to it. The temperature outside had plummeted, and the streets were quiet.

No one was around. Not a soul. Not a sound.

Whatever hit Cleveland left it virtually unrecognizable. There were no discerning landmarks, nor reference of direction.

Harris stated, almost in shock, "Just go right. Make a right. I always turned right when I walked out of the building."

"Then what?" Marissa asked.

"Then we keep going in the hope we get a sense of direction."

"So, does this mean we're sticking together?" Marissa questioned.

"Just until we get out of the city."

Toby couldn't believe that was such a concern for Marissa. If Harris wanted to be on his own, then that was fine with Toby. It was his loss not theirs.

But how could either one of them even think about anything else but what had happened to Cleveland?

The broken buildings were not the extent of it. Everything was black. Soot and grime covered everything. The amount of charred bodies matched the degree of rubble. They scattered about everywhere, under concrete, curled in balls, some tossed to the side and some in pieces. Frozen in time, instantly burnt to a crisp. They weren't the only human remains. There were the remains forever embedded on any wall left standing. Another horrific testament to the human loss. The force of the bombs was so strong they not only incinerated the people, they created a photograph of them, in the form of a shadow on the wall.

Toby had seen pictures of such an event when it happened in Hiroshima. He always wondered what it was. A burn mark, ashes, remains?

He had to know.

Pausing, Toby reached out to a wall and trailed his fingers on the image of a head. After he rolled his fingers together, there was nothing on them and the image hadn't smeared.

It was all that remained of person who, a little more than a week earlier, had a life, a family. Now they were a mere etched-in-stone image and a gruesome historical marking.

The goal was to get out of the city, to the outskirts, where hopefully there would be people and help.

Slowly and surely, with very few words between them, they did their best to get from the circumference of ground zero Cleveland.

## Swall, CA – San Joaquin Valley

The pump was doing its job, but Joe only ran it a small amount of time per day. Despite the chic discrete design boasted by Mike's Well Service, it still let out a racket when it was really rolling. It was one of four on his property and the best producing well he had. He kept the pump in a small well house that looked more like a taller dog house.

The other wells, he didn't bother hiding their production, but this one he did. It was his supply well. Each day he'd run it during the late morning, load a bunch of gallon containers in his truck and drive the quarter mile across his property to the canning operations building.

Outside it looked like a newer barn, and inside was where Joe's workers made his trademark Fat Joe's tomatoes.

It was quiet in there. Not a single employee or piece of machinery was running. A few hours earlier it was noisy. Joe was producing a carton of canned goods. Cook the tomatoes, jar them, seal them, and stick them in a box. After he finished, he shut down, cleaned up, and aired the place out.

It had become his new daily routine. Canning and then water.

He was just about finished with that before heading out to the fields.

He had returned from the water pump to the barn. Joe moved a mat, lifted the floorboard under steamer number three and exposed a staircase. He carried the water down and placed it against the far wall.

The downstairs storage area was filling up nicely. Soon he would be well stocked. He needed it to be that way. Word of the resistance had reached him and he knew those foot soldiers fighting for freedom would need a safe place, one stocked with provisions, so they could hide away, rest, and gain strength for the battles.

That was Joe's plan. His contribution to the cause. He wasn't in shape enough to fight. He would if he had to, but his part would be to keep the soldiers strong.

He was stockpiling nicely and secretively. Even though the invaders had set up a headquarters in San Joaquin Valley with the mayor perched on their lap, no one had even approached him or visited his farm.

That was about to change.

He pulled the string on the light and as he started up the stairs he heard the sound of motors, a truck motor. He hurried, shut the floor hatch, covered it with the mat, and peeked out the window. Sure enough, a jeep and a truck were parked outside.

Figuring he might as well see what the visit was about, he left his canning building.

Four foreign soldiers stepped from the truck, and from the jeep an Asian man wearing a suit accompanied the mayor. Joe had never met him before personally but knew his face.

Mumbling under his breath, "Snitch," Joe took a breath and placed on a fake smile. "Morning, gentlemen, what can I do for you?"

"We are looking for Mr. Fajo," the Asian gentleman said.

"Excuse me?" Joe asked.

"Mr. Fajo."

"Fajo?"

"Yes."

"Oh." Joe chuckled. "Fat Joe."

"Yes. Fajo."

"Not Fajo. Fat Joe. Fat ..." He patted his stomach. "Joe. Fat Joe. Get it?"

"No."

"I used to be large. Fat Joe is a nickname and now a trade name. My name is Joe Garbino. Anyhow ... what's up?" Joe asked.

"You are a large producer in the area," he said. "We have reason to believe that you may be ... what is the word?"

The mayor stepped forward. "Hoarding. They'd like to check the property."

"Hoarding?" Joe asked with ridicule. "Why in the world would you think that? I mean you are welcome to check but, come on, hoarding?"

"Joe," the mayor said. "You didn't drop your Wednesday order off at the school or Mavis'. You also didn't show up at UPS to ship out."

"First of all, who the hell knew UPS was still running.

Secondly ... I don't stockpile, my orders are made fresh and shipped out the same week. From farm to can in hours, that's my motto. My farm is dying. Because right now I only pick what I can eat. As far as production, how the hell am I gonna do that without any workers? You wanna know why nothing has gone out? I ain't had anyone here to work."

The suited gentleman looked at the mayor for clarification.

"He's not hoarding. He's not producing right now," the mayor said.

The suited gentleman looked around. "He has a large farm."

"Yep." Joe nodded. "I do."

"You must produce."

"Oh, I produce the food," Joe said. "I just can't produce the Fat Joe product. You're welcome to go out to the fields and get whatever you want. Otherwise it will rot on the vine. In case you didn't know, war broke out and my employees never came back to work."

"How many hand workers do you need to produce your normal quantity?" he asked.

"I lost sixteen employees."

The suited man nodded. "You will have twenty tomorrow. The liberation movement will pay their wages and will compensate you for the products. But you will produce what is asked of you."

"Will they be my workers?" Joe asked.

"They will be workers."

"Will they know what they're doing? Trained?"

"If not, you will train them." He turned and walked back to the jeep. "But you will deliver the orders."

"You mean fill my standing orders?" Joe asked.

The suited gentleman ignored him but the mayor answered.

"No," said the mayor. "You will be given a quota to deliver daily."

"Daily?" Joe barked. "My system is set up for weekly."

"Then I suggest you change."

"Change what?" Joe argued. "My system? You're sending me workers that may or may not know what they're doing. Not only do I have to push them, I have to train them. Weekly? You'll bleed this farm dry."

"I doubt that. You'll keep up. If you need more workers, let us know. But you will produce daily." The mayor walked to the jeep as well.

Joe stood there watching as they backed up and the truck and jeep drove away. At least they didn't search his property, his stash under the warehouse would remain hidden. That didn't make things any better. He had no idea what they would want him to produce. A part of Joe feared it was going to not only be a hard quota to fill but one that would interfere with his underground movement plan. However, it wouldn't stop it. He'd figure out how he'd get things done. In the meantime, he'd break his routine and do an afternoon of production just in case it was going to be a few days until he could stock his private stash. Before that, he headed back to the house. He wanted to call Saul and see if he received a visit and demand on his strawberry farm. If not, he was going to give Saul the heads up. It was only a matter of time before they showed up. The foreign invaders were making it known they claimed the land and that included their farms.

# Chapter Eight

## Hanlen, WV

There was never an instance in his life, at least that Cal could remember, when he felt so sick. Maybe he did and just forgot, but he couldn't recall feeling as bad as he did, lying on a cot in a packed high-school gym.

His chest was sore and black and blue, the nurse told him that was from them doing a cardiac thump on him. He felt weak and short of breath, and to top that all off, he couldn't keep anything down or in him.

If he wasn't leaning over a basin, he was asking for help changing the bed pan.

The odor was horrendous, not just from him but from everyone else around him.

Cal wasn't special. Not there, not when the closest sick person in proximity to him was an arm's reach away. At least he was grateful that he wasn't seeing any blood in his regurgitation unlike the poor man next to him. All that man brought up was blood and it smelled putrid.

The guy's face was spotted with a burn on his cheek. His arms were blackened with what looked like bruises and his hair was thin and scarce.

Cal wondered what he looked like but dared not to ask for a mirror.

He just wanted to get better. To stop floating in and out of consciousness and find his friends, find … Louise.

When Leana searched for them, all she could report to Cal was that all of them were being treated for radiation sickness.

"It's not a short game," she told him. "You're not gonna feel better in a few days. It's not the flu. And you especially will take a while. You're recovering on many levels."

It wasn't like Cal to just do nothing, sick or not. From his cot, he watched the number of workers dwindle. The healthcare worker to patient ratio used to be good, but over a period of a few days, he only saw one and Leana wasn't the worker.

What happened to her? Was she alright?

While he tried to focus on the goings-on of the aid station, he drifted off again.

The brief slumber bred a vivid dream. The wedding that never happened, all the guests, the purple and gold decorations. Staring at his beautiful wife. When he woke, at first, he believed the entire war, the bombs, the sickness was all part of a dream. They weren't. Just as he started to close his eyes again, he saw the lone healthcare worker struggling with a patient and Cal decided, sick or not, he couldn't lie there and do nothing.

With a grunt he sat up slowly and swung his legs over the side of the cot. He took a moment, let the dizziness subside before he stood.

When his feet touched the ground he swayed left to right nearly losing his balance. Hand to the cot, he caught himself. He wasn't attached to an IV and that was a good thing. He took a deep breath and slowly, nursing the cots as a crutch, made his way to the healthcare worker.

Cal couldn't tell if the patient was a man or woman, only that the worker, who was male, was having a hard time.

The patient thrust up and down, legs kicking. The worker was trying to secure the legs, give some sort of medication while pleading with the patient to be calm.

The closer Cal drew the clearer he saw that the bedding was a mess and so was the floor. Smeared with blood and bodily fluids, Cal brought his hand to his mouth as he made it even closer.

The stench of rotten bile burned his nostrils

"Calm, please, I just want to help you," the healthcare worker said.

"Here," Cal said as he made his approach. "Let me. Hold

them down, I'll inject. I don't have the strength."

"Thank you so …" The worker peered over his shoulder and saw Cal. "No, get back in bed. You shouldn't be up."

"I can't … I can't just lay there."

"Yes, you can."

"No … I can't. What can I do to help?"

Exasperated, the worker exhaled in defeat. "Here." He handed Cal a syringe. "Just inject it in the thigh. Do it fast, I'll only be able to hold her down so long."

Cal nodded and stepped forward. He could see the woman's legs were frail and thin, covered with sores that bled and looked bruised. When he made it directly to the cot, he saw her arms were the same, and she shook her head violently. Her head was void of hair and covered with brown birth-like burn marks.

"Get ready," the worker said.

Cal prepared to deliver the medication. He watched as the worker secured her legs. When that happened, Cal froze.

"Now. Right now," the worker ordered.

It took a second for Cal to snap out of it and he plunged the contents of the syringe into the thigh, then stepped back and froze again.

He couldn't move, couldn't think. His heart dropped to the pit of his stomach when he saw poor woman wasn't a stranger … it was Louise.

# Charleston, WV

It was something Madeline didn't expect to feel … guilt. Not for being taken as a prisoner of war, but she felt guilty because she was relieved.

She tried to rationalize the relief, but it was hard. She was leader of the free world, which was no longer free. She wasn't supposed to be relieved she was captured. Yet, she was.

There was a sense to her that it was over.

The invasion, the war, even the domestic terror strikes, were a lot for an experienced sitting president to handle. Madeline was tossed into the fray, full body and mind, and there wasn't a solid plan. They couldn't even come up with one because there was no way to know what was going on.

She was stuck in an old cold war era bunker, wearing a military uniform that was far too big for her. She was cold, hungry, tired, and confused. She hated herself for it.

Given the time, Madeline would have come up with a strategy. Now, that was time was done.

She was taken, like the queen in a game of chess.

Madeline didn't know where they were taking her. She raised her arms because she didn't want a shot fired, she didn't want her men and women at the bunker hurt. She assumed those who were there would be taken as well.

There were two trucks and she was loaded into the back of one alone.

It was when the truck began to roll away that she heard the shots fired, the explosion. She closed her eyes and wanted to cry. Her yielding to the soldiers was for naught, they hit the bunker anyhow.

Troy and the others were more than likely gone. Madeline was the only surviving member of the senate or congress, that she knew about.

She was now a prisoner of war.

The one voice to represent the fight and defense was silenced and in the back of a truck.

With each mile she rode the more she realized, there would be no battle, no fighting back, no conquering the enemy.

It was over.

In fact, it was pretty much over the second the enemy landed on American soil.


They drove for a while, at least an hour. She couldn't see where they were. Madeline wasn't shackled or handcuffed, nor was she treated roughly. She was escorted by two armed guards who didn't speak to her at all.

When the truck stopped, the curtain in the back opened and her armed guards stood there. They offered her assistance in getting down and that was when she saw she was at an airport.

It was a short walk from the truck to the aircraft, a private jet with no name on it.

"Where am I going?" she asked. "Where are you taking me?"

She wasn't sure what she expected, maybe it was shock that had kept her from speaking up earlier. Instantly, she panicked. Her pace slowed and her footing became more resistant. They led her more than before and inched her up the outer staircase through the open door of the plane. The engines were already running and warming up.

The interior of the plane was beautiful, clean, and comfortable. Eight rows of wide white leather seats lined one side of the plane, and on the other was a sofa and table. Her escorts left as soon as they got her inside.

Madeline's heart raced.

A few moments later a female flight attendant came out, dressed in a crisp uniform, and pointed to a seat.

"Where are we going?" Madeline asked. "Where are you taking me?"

The flight attendant smiled and pointed to the seats.

After a brief pause, Madeline took a seat and the attendant handed her a soft blanket. As soon as she sat, she closed her eyes. The seat was comfortable and warm. The blanket felt wonderful. The flight attendant left and returned with a cup of coffee and a warm wet towel that smelled of lemon. She placed them both on the small table area next to Madeline's seat.

Madeline grabbed the towel and placed it on her face, then after it cooled, she set it down and lifted the coffee.

The guilt returned when she took a sip. It felt like ages since she'd had a cup of coffee.

She had to remember what was happening. She was taken during a siege, yet, Madeline didn't contest. It wasn't that she was weak, she was just at a loss.

There was no point in arguing or putting up a fight because she didn't know anything. She was in the dark. She had no clue who had taken her and where they were headed. It had to be all part of the process.

A foreign country had invaded.

She was the leader.

In fact, there was nothing she could do except drink her coffee and wait and see where she landed. Hopefully then, someone would talk to her and tell her what was going on.

## Cleveland, OH

It was a great place to stop for the night, in fact, Toby found it and called it irony. It was one of the few remaining intact buildings on the outskirts of Cleveland. A wholistic healer of Western

Medicine. The windows weren't busted and just inside the small building was the reception area. It was a cross between a store and waiting room.

The back had examining tables which made a great place to sleep.

Toby walked a good twenty feet ahead of Marissa and Harris. He was the scout, keeping an eye out. They wanted to find a car, but any that were viable didn't have keys or gas and none of them were savvy enough to get one working.

When Toby realized the day was winding down he started looking for a stopping place.

They had made it out of the city on a south-bound path. Harris would stay with them until they reached his home, then he was stopping while Toby and Marissa went west.

Harris was convinced that everything was fine once they cleared the perimeter of Cleveland and the destruction. That somehow there were rescue crews abound, walking and searching.

Toby knew that wasn't the case, or at least they weren't nearby. He didn't hear any dogs and that was the telltale sign to Toby no one was out there. Rescue workers, that was.

They did see a few people who, like themselves, were walking south. They met a woman and her two young boys. They looked dirty and tired, the youngest boy looked ill.

Convinced help was not far away, Harris gave them water and

food from his ration. He claimed that he didn't need them, rations were probably plenty outside of Cleveland.

They had however cleared the worst part of destruction, and the farther they walked the more buildings they saw.

Even he knew it was a limited strike and wasn't like the entire country had been blasted away. They just needed to get out of the area and see what was happening with the world.

For that night, they were staying put.

Toby closed the window blinds, had some of his food, rummaged through what the store had that was useful, then went to the back to turn in for the night.

None of them said much at all that night.

He was the first to wake up. The health store had protein bars and he had one of those. It was when he was gathering his stuff that he heard the sound of a truck. It sounded like a big one, too.

When he heard it, his immediate thought was that maybe Harris was right.

"Dudes, get up," he told them. "I am hearing trucks outside. I'm gonna go check it out."

Harris immediately jumped up and Toby raced out before he saw if Marissa woke.

Once outside he caught a glimpse of the large truck. It was military and Toby smiled, running back in.

"It's the military," he said. "Harris, looks like you might be right. They're probably looking for people."

Instantly they grabbed their gear and raced out. The sound of the truck had faded, but they were hopeful.

"We need to get out into the open," Harris suggested. "We veered off the main road. Which way did the truck go?"

Toby pointed and Harris took off in that direction.

They followed as Harris walked at a strong, quick pace. They walked for a good half an hour until they found a road. It was a four-lane main road, not a highway.

Cars had stopped and been abandoned on the side of the road. They looked as if they had been moved aside.

They stayed center of the road, completely visible. Within a half an hour, the sound of a truck carried to them.

It came from behind and was getting close.

Toby looked over his shoulder and saw it coming. It didn't look like it was slowing down at all.

The three of them stepped to the side and waved their arms, calling out, "Stop. Help."

Just as the truck past them about fifty feet, it came to a stop.

Marissa smiled, Harris showed excitement, and Toby did a little skip and jump.

It was one of those long green military trucks with a tarp canopy covering the entire back. They quickly made their way to the truck and as soon as they got there, relieved and slightly out of breath, the back gate dropped, the tarp opened, and two Chinese soldiers jumped out, aiming their weapons at them.

"What the hell?" Harris asked.

"Bags. Bags. Down," one soldier said. "Hands up."

Toby did as instructed, dropping his bags and raising his hands. Once Harris and Marissa did the same, the soldier swung his weapon and pointed to the truck.

"In," he ordered. "In now."

Toby didn't have a clue what was going on, or why Asian soldiers had guns on them. He did as he was told, he would have believed that maybe China came to help if he didn't have a gun in his face.

As soon as Toby was close to the back gate of the truck, he knew they weren't rescuers and they were in trouble. The inside of the back end of the truck was filled with people, all looking scared and all of them Americans.

## Outskirts of Houston, TX

He was tired. His journey from his homeland to America had been nonstop and long, but General Liu wasn't ready to stop, he couldn't. He relaxed on the plane, taking the time to look over his area and the plans laid out for him.

He hated it.

If his country was to put on the appearance of being humanitarian and helping America, the detention camps were not the way to do so.

His folder stated his area had already initiated nine detention camps. Four of which were filled to capacity. They were wasting valuable resources and manpower detaining people. People they had to feed, house, and guard. That wasn't including the camps erected for those who were displaced. Americans who had lost their homes to the bombs and were seeking refuge and answers. In his opinion, it was an undertaking that was too large.

There was no inkling of war, nothing to suggest that China would attack and invade the United States. The only reason he could think of was the recent tariffs that hurt their country. Not to mention the tax placed on imports of food.

All of those were negotiable items, not war worthy.

He was supposed to go to San Antonio, his base of operation. Instead, he needed to see something he never thought he would see in his lifetime: the devastating effects of a nuclear weapon on a large American city. The George Bush International Airport was unaffected by the bombs, at least the runways were. He set a course for that. Fen Shu wasn't happy and expressed her dismay. General Liu didn't care. He set a course to land at that airport after circling around Houston.

When they did, he couldn't believe it and couldn't take his

eyes off it.

The gleaming city of Houston which was spread across a flat terrain, encircled by its intricate wide roadways, took the brunt force of the nuclear weapons.

The bomb had hit dead center causing a massive crater that ate most of the city and buildings. The outer area of the crater was rubble and the roadways were twisted wreckage.

A thin cloud lingered in the area hiding a lot of damage, but General Liu didn't need to see fully to know what had happened and what was left.

The air was deemed safe enough for short term exposure with low level readings of radiation, and General Liu ordered that they land.

"I don't understand why it is we are landing," Fen said.

"This area is devastated. I need to see what we are doing with those who have survived."

"Minimal. There is not much we can do without a surrender."

"There were two million people that lived in this area, and you tell me we are doing minimal?"

"It is all part of the plan. If we take care of them their hands will not be forced for a surrender. Right now, the Americans are setting up their own medical camps. We are merely overseeing them."

"Then I need to see what we have done."

Once they landed, a car waited for them. Fen repeatedly expressed that it was not part of his job but the general disagreed. If he was to control an area, he needed to know everything that he had to control.

The first medical station they visited was located not far from the Houston epicenter. The People's Republic of China was present, but mainly it was an American set up.

At least two dozen large white tents were erected, and in the field surrounding that, hundreds of people camped out. This was their home.

They were shouted at, spat at, and even had items thrown at them as they walked into the medical area.

The Americans made it clear they were not welcome.

Liu looked at every person he passed. All of them began looking the same. Dirty faces, some had injuries that were not healing. People lay on blankets and in the grass. Their faces expressed loss, hurt, and anger.

The first tent they entered, Fen left immediately. The smell was horrendous, rotting, burnt, and sour. Liu took a mask and covered his mouth and nose, though it did little to cover the smell.

The large tent was packed with cots and every single one of them was occupied.

He walked through, looking at the victims, many of them burned, missing limbs. Some too sick to even move while only a handful of healthcare workers moved about.

He walked through that tent and into the next.

That one was different. Even though it was just as packed it had a quieter feel to it. Those in that tent didn't seem to be injured, they were different, and he noticed it right away when he looked upon a man who lay on his side. The man coughed out of control and turned left to right as if he were trying desperately to get comfortable. His skin was pale, glistening with a layer of sweat, but the entire area around his nose and mouth was covered with sores. General Liu slowed down and looked at the man. Not only was it his face, but his hands had the same sores.

He turned to the cot next to the man and the person there, a woman, looked the same.

Something was wrong.

Immediately, he started to visually examine the patients. They all looked the same: sores, pale, sweaty, and the general then sought out someone on the medical team that was helping them.

His English was pretty good, and he approached a woman wearing scrubs. "These people here. What is this? Radiation? They don't look like the others."

The woman ignored him and kept moving.

Frustrated, he followed the woman. "I am speaking to you."

She spun around. "I don't care. I'm busy. I'm taking care of people you … you and your people hurt."

"These people are victims of the bombs?" he asked. "They do not look it. This looks like sickness."

"It is."

"From the bombs?"

"I doubt that," she replied. "These people survived the blast and the radiation."

"Then what is it?"

"Why don't you tell me," she said. "Because they all just started coming in two days ago not long after you arrived. I guess the few bombs weren't enough. It's no coincidence that some sort of virus is now out of control. So why don't you tell me what you brought? So we can try to help these people."

General Liu didn't have an answer.

"If this interests you, move on to the next tent, there's another two hundred there. And take a deep breath, maybe you'll get it."

Before he could respond, she had moved on.

She had to be mistaken. If he understood her correctly, she was accusing and blaming the invasion for an outbreak, some sort of biological warfare. To the best of his knowledge that wasn't part of the plan, not at all. Then again, with Fen Shu at the helm, he couldn't be all that certain that they hadn't brought the disease to America. Thinking about what Fen had said, make America weak and needy, a deadly viral outbreak would be the thing that would do just that. He had to wonder even as cold and callous as she was, would she do something as inhumane as that? There was only one way to find out, he would ask. In the meantime, he would move the supplies required to the medical station to get the sick the help they needed. That was the least he could do.

# CHAPTER NINE

## Thirteen Days Post Bombs

## White Sulphur Springs, WV

The smoke that trickled into the communications room wasn't alarming as much as it was irritating. Troy wasn't thinking at first. He believed that it was perhaps some wire burning, something simple. He told Madeline to leave, but he didn't expect her to leave the shelter.

She was escorted out and Troy figured it was to the other level. After all, the bunker was a contained environment.

After radioing and tracing the source of the smoke, Troy had a bad feeling. What if the enemy tapped into their location and was using the outside ventilation to smoke them out? Immediately, he went into lockdown, closing and securing all bunker doors, both interior and tunnel entrances. No one was getting in. Every entrance was closed. The lockdown was protected by a two-person number system.

It was when he returned to get the president that he realized she was outside. By the time he had Major Reyes put in his code, the ground shook with explosions.

Troy's heart raced out of control. What had he done? He sent out the president into the madness.

Six minutes.

It was a lifetime.

Six minutes it took to open the doors, arm up, and charge out.

He led the troops.

Racing up the tunnel entrance he could hear the gunfire. It was steady, in the distance, and then just as he reached topside, it slowed down like popping corn.

He emerged to fire.

The beautiful grounds had been set aflame, the once grand, white Greenbrier Resort ... burned. The entire left wing was engulfed in flames and thick black smoke billowed up into the air.

He had over twenty men on the perimeter, and body parts scattered about.

Every vehicle they had outside was destroyed.

He could hear screaming, and Troy charged toward them.

One of his soldiers was trapped in a burning truck. His hands pounded against the smoky glass. The door had been jammed and Troy jumped on the hood of the burning vehicle, smashed the windshield, and pulled out the driver.

He died within seconds.

"No, no, no!" Troy cried out. How could he be so stupid? How could he let it happen?

She was gone.

One lone soldier stationed on the exterior lived.

"They took her," he said. "They took her, put her in the truck, and shot the two men with her."

Defeated was an understatement. He was tasked with the job of keeping the president safe and he failed.

Troy's next move was to find her. He also had to abandon the bunker; he didn't know if the enemy would be back or not.

He and his remaining men, all seventy of them, gathered every weapon they could, bagged supplies and water, and hit the road. They divided up. Some went south toward Charleston. Troy went north. He figured that was where they had reports of invading troops. They would have to take her close.


Two days into the journey, exhausted from walking, wounds failing to heal, Troy spotted an orange flyer posted on a telephone pole outside a rest stop.

It was oddly placed, almost as if it wasn't supposed to be there and Troy knew as soon as he saw it, that the flyer was coded.

It had to be.

To him it screamed a call to arms, a recruitment for a re-sistance. Something Troy was wanting to do.

With that flyer in hand, he radioed his men that had headed south and then, with his group, headed to the location on that flyer.


## Hanlen, WV


When Cal was in secondary school, he had a class called Personal and Social Education. They were doing a study on war and effects on society, and as preparation for the class discussion Cal watched two movies. Both were on nuclear war and both of them made during the height of the cold war era. They weren't propaganda, they were a hard look at would could happen.

While the American movie, *The Day After*, really was medi-cally informative, the BBC drama, *Threads*, scared the hell out of him so much that he had forgotten all about the American film. *Threads* was horrific; it dealt with the blast aftermath and the downfall of society.

And in the aftermath of his own personal confrontation with nuclear war, Cal was ready to kick himself for forgetting those movies.

How could he do so? He debated those movies in class, he had nightmares. Yet for some reason, knowing full well nuclear weapons had exploded by him, everything he learned from those films remained hidden in the file cabinet of his mind until he ended up on a cot in the medical camp.

Suddenly, upon looking around, he was in that final gymnasium scene of *The Day After*. Scores of people lying on cots and whatever they could find. The hero of the movie, limping his way to his love interest ravaged by radiation. All of it could have been avoided had he remembered an inkling of what he saw in those movies. Had he done so he would have insisted on finding shelter, at least for a week. None of them would be ill.

The effects on his body should not have come as a shock to him. He knew better. There was no one to blame for his ignorance.

Back then, when he watched them, nuclear war was a thing of the past. A relic of an age gone by, pretty much a fable that would never happen. However, there he was making his way to Louise.

He hobbled across the gym floor, stepping over sick people. Victims of war, fleeing from their home cities that were hit. Refugees hoping to find a safe haven became incapacitated, radiated statistics stuck in a high-school gym.

Just like Louise.

Cal made it his personal job to take care of her. Several times a day he tended to her, fed her, washed her, changed her, and at the end of the day, he sat with her. More than anything he wanted to move her somewhere private, but there was nowhere to move her. Not yet. Once she was better and didn't need constant attention and IV treatment, Cal could move her to a classroom.

Then again, there was little medical help available. One doctor, two nurses and a few volunteers. That was it. There was news and chatter on the radio that help was coming. However, that seemed like a fairy tale as supplies diminished.

There were positives.

Cal didn't look nearly as bad as he felt.

He successfully avoided his reflection fearing he'd look like one of those stricken in the *The Day After*, or from the multitudes of images he had scene from Hiroshima. Surprisingly, he wasn't as bad as his mind imagined. He wore a baseball cap to cover his balding head, his weight loss wasn't as drastic as many, and he didn't have the radiation birthmark-like discoloration that many had. His radiated wounds were healing and he hadn't lost his teeth. Something many of those in the gym had experienced. Their teeth just fell out.

Shortly after Cal gathered the strength to stand and help, he discovered Jake and Ricky. Since both of them weren't nearly as bad as Cal, he encouraged them to get up and get moving.

They did.

Cal was convinced that staying busy was what made him feel better.

The three of them were quickly educated on what to do.

Cal learned a lot, how to do an IV, change a bandage, however, the tooth loss was one of the last things he learned.

He was sitting at a table with Jake and Ricky, sipping on broth when he noticed Jake fiddling with a tooth.

"What are you doing?" Cal asked.

"It's loose, man," Jake replied.

"Did you hit it in the accident?"

"I don't think so. It's just loose."

Ricky looked up from his meal. "It's the radiation. It causes your gums to recede and your teeth to fall out."

"No way," Cal said.

"Yep." Jake removed his fingers from his mouth and between them was his front tooth. "Just came right out."

Cal cringed.

Jake dropped the tooth and it 'clinked' against the plate.

"Don't …" Cal winced. "Pick that up."

"I lost three yesterday," Ricky said. "See." He flashed a smile to show the spaces.

Immediately Cal checked his teeth. They felt strong, but he prepared for the worst. He only hoped he could handle it as nonchalant as Jake and Ricky. Their reasoning was that it was better to be toothless and alive then dead with perfect pearly whites.

Cal told that to Louise who, although tried to put on the face of being strong, cringed with a simple sip of water because her mouth hurt so badly. Her gums bled and her lips were swollen.

She was alive and her chances of living increased every day she held on.

That day Cal stood from the cot was the day that the doctor believed Louise was going to die. She had a ninety percent chance. But she made it through that day, and each day increased her odds of survival.

Louise shunned Cal at first.

*Leave me alone.*

*Let me die.*

*Don't look at me.*

Then she relented, accepted his help, and welcomed his care over that from a stranger.

Cal was bound and determined to see her through.

Before it all, Louise was a strong woman, outspoken and full of life. It broke Cal's heart to see her so weak. He didn't baby her or pamper her, he pushed her to fight.

She was a fighter before and needed to be one now.

Louise would get there, Cal was certain.

She wasn't his only patient on this day. Cal had a third of the floor. Nearly twenty of his patients had to be aided in eating.

Louise was always first and foremost. He fed her even when she fought him on it. He made sure she ate and had water. If he couldn't be by her side, he had Ricky or Jake be there. When of course, they weren't out making runs, looking for supplies. As soon as they could, they went out.

Cal was envious. Even though he was getting better, he still lacked a lot of strength.

On this day, he washed and smelled fresh. He sported the cap that Jake had found for him and wore a clean shirt.

Louise noticed and said he "smelled good" but wasn't feeling much for food. A few sips of water and she forced a smile of gratitude as Cal moistened her lips.

She wanted to try to sit up, but Cal asked her to wait one more day.

"Will I make it one more day?" she asked.

"Of course," Cal replied. "You made it this far, right? You're strong. You'll beat this thing."

"What's going on out there, Cal?" she asked.

"What do you mean?"

"With the attacks. What's going on? Who did this?"

Cal opened his mouth to reply but stopped. He didn't know. He honestly didn't know. In fact, he hadn't thought of the logistics of what had happened and who did what. His knowledge of what occurred was limited to what was happening in that gym. He was certain he didn't want to know and didn't want to face that reality yet. Because if things were that bad in the little West Virginia middle-of-nowhere high-school gym, he couldn't imagine how bad it was everywhere else.

# CHAPTER TEN

## San Antonio, TX

A wonderful warm meal was served on the plane and Madeline sipped on an alcoholic beverage which calmed her nerves. She had no idea where she was even after they landed. She had sat on the plane hours after they landed until it was night and had then been escorted out and placed in a windowless room off a large hanger. There inside was a cot, fresh towels, a change of clothes that consisted of tan drawstring pants and a long sleeve T-shirt. In the room was a small powder room with running water. A notebook and pen sat on the folding TV tray table next to a lamp. It was simple, plain, and she was in that room for days. The only human contact she had was twice a day when they brought her a meal.

Then finally, they came for her. It was the first time she had seen daylight in a while and her eyes hurt and had to adjust. They placed her in a car with heavily tinted windows and when she arrived at her destination, she learned the location.

Had it been a mistake?

She wasn't expecting her final stop.

Madeline knew it to be one of the finest, if not *the* finest hotel in San Antonio. They rushed her from the door into the hotel. The lobby had extremely high ceilings, tall windows, and white square pillars. The green block carpet mixed with marble set off the eloquent furnishings.

Immediately she was placed into an elevator and taken to the highest floor. She paused before entering the room. She may have been stepping into a grand hotel, but the brand-new, shiny lock added to the exterior of the door told her she was to make no mistake, she was still a prisoner.

The soldier nudged her into a huge suite with a window overlooking the city

A timid housekeeper stepped forward. She was American.

"Madam President." She nodded. "They have taken the liberty of providing you with suitable clothing. You will find them in the closet and dresser. Should sizes be an issue, let us know."

"Who?" Madeline asked. "Who is doing this?"

"Enjoy your stay. I will check back tomorrow. I am to tell you, someone will be here in an hour to speak to you."

"Who? Who, dear?"

She rushed out, and the soldier followed. The door closed, and Madeline heard them locking it. Just to double check, she tried the handle, it wouldn't budge.

The conveniences were there and Madeline took advantage. She showered, scrubbing her skin until it was sore. She found an outfit that fit, and when she emerged from the dressing area, she was greeted by a younger Asian woman, well dressed with a staunch demeanor.

"American President," she said. "Allow me to introduce myself. I am agent Fen Shu, I am the head of the organization that is much like your CIA."

"I am surprised they sent an agent. I would expect a military leader or ambassador."

"Why is that?" Fen asked. "I am in charge and overseeing all ground base operations. I am the ambassador, if you will." She paced slowly, her hands folded behind her back. "You are wondering now why you are here."

Madeline nodded.

"We are not savages. You are a leader and deserve fitting accommodations. But you are in our custody."

"A prisoner of war," Madeline said.

"How can you be a prisoner of war?" Fen asked. "What war?" She walked to the large window in the living room of the suite. "Look out. It's a beautiful day. I see no signs of war."

"Maybe not here." Madeline walked near her. "Out there are signs. Cities hit with nuclear bombs. Your soldiers with a massive land invasion."

"Yes, we have arrived, but we didn't start this thing."

"The hell you didn't."

"The hell we did," Fen argued. "Your people did. Your people opened the door when they decided to divide the country, to render it powerless, even just briefly. That act of terror was an invitation. One we took. And we are here to make things right." Fen walked away from the window.

"Why did you take me?"

"You were communicating outside the country. We tracked that signal. You also are the leader. How can you lead two hundred feet underground? To me, and many others, it was as if you were hiding? What leader hides?"

"I had no choice."

"There is always a choice. You have a choice now. Your country is crumbling. We can only do so much to help you. Many are injured, starving, homeless. Is this the country you want to lead? A good leader knows when it is time to step back. Madam President, this is your opportunity to show the world what kind of leader you really are."

"I don't understand," Madeline said.

"Actually, I believe you do. You just don't realize it yet." Fen walked across the room, toward the door. She paused at the television. "You may turn this on. You can see what other countries are saying. You can see footage we are taking for you. Please, enjoy. Life shall be easy for you in here, unlike out there."

"Then let me out," Madeline said.

"We will. When you make the choice."

"Aw, yes, the choice," Madeline said sarcastically. "The one I am supposed to know about. Spit it out, Ms. Shu. What do you want from me?"

"Simple." After a pause, Fen replied, "Your surrender. You need to surrender your country. You need to do what's best. Now is your time to shine. Watch the television. Think about it. You're not going anywhere until you do." She opened the door and smiled. "Good day."

Madeline didn't even know where to begin. Surrender? It seemed absurd to her to surrender, to give up the fight before they even had a chance to engage.

Madeline wasn't ready to give up the country, not yet. Not until she knew for sure and without a doubt that it was the only option.

## Holly River Base, WV

The flyer was slightly crumbled and damp when Troy put it on the table before Gus. "I saw this. I'm hoping this isn't just a fishing tournament."

"It's not," Gus said.

"Good. I got about forty men hiding in the woods, waiting to know if this is safe."

"It's safe."

"Thank you, sir." Troy gave a nod of respect, turned, and walked out.

The management cabin of the vacation area was the first check point for those joining the rebellion and cause. Two men worked there constantly, one behind the counter and the other in the backroom, headphones on, monitoring messages sent via Morse Code.

If anyone arrived, such as the man who identified himself as Troy, whoever was at the desk would sound off a moose horn. The noise would carry through the valley and either Gus or Steve would make their way up the one-mile path.

When Troy arrived, he showed his military ID. He was still in uniform but looked worse for wear. Dirty, bruised, and tired. After he walked out to retrieve his men, Gus told the check in man, "Send them down. I'll get them situated and acclimated."

"Got it. We didn't unpack the truck of tents yet," the young man said.

"We'll get to it."

Holding that crinkled flyer, Gus headed back to base. He could hear the sound of running water, but very few voices. No loud sounds were permitted; they were under the radar and wanted to stay that way.

Steve had made it half way up the path as Gus walked back.

"Everything okay?" Steve asked.

Gus handed him the flyer. "Another forty on their way down. These ones all soldiers as well."

"Christ, Gus, where we gonna put them?"

"We have enough room. We'll figure it out. Besides, I want to move the first group out."

"Where to?"

"Something easy. Obtainable victory so we can keep momentum."

"Proc Checkpoint. Breezewood?" Steve asked.

"That's what I'm thinking. We've waited long enough. It's time …" Gus said. "It's time we start the fight."

## Bern, Switzerland

Russian President Petrov initiated the meeting, called all the leaders personally, and accepted Switzerland's invitation to host.

A part of him should have known better. The joke about Switzerland being neutral wasn't just a joke, it did have merit behind it.

Petrov was in one of the fortunate countries. He was able to keep it together and amped up the military presence before things went awry.

The summit was more of a meeting, a large conference table with only a few countries in attendance. China did not show and they continued to deny any wrongdoing.

Petrov, along with the leaders of Great Britain, Australia, and Canada offered documentation to the others in the room. Information they were already aware of.

The point of the meeting was to collectively decide what could be done. Clearly the events in the United States were affecting the global community.

After three hours of discussing the situation, when they returned from a short break, it was over before Petrov knew it.

Everyone voiced their concerns.

"And what does this have to do with us?" asked Switzerland.

"We will give humanitarian aid, but no more than that," said Japan.

"There's no reason, if China has taken over, that we cannot work the same deal as we did with United States," said Germany.

The general consensus was … it was a new order, and let it go.

The responses were echoed around the room and as they filed out one by one, Petrov wanted more than anything to storm out. But he didn't. He stayed. Wallowing in that room in defeat and an abundance of worry.

It seemed everyone had their own problems, which were valid, and they couldn't be bothered, nor did they have the energy or resources to deal with what was happening in the United States. They all seemed to want to take the path of least resistance and damage. What would end the crisis soon. What would put everything back on the right path?

It was understandable, no one ever really wanted to have a military interference. But sometimes, it was necessary.

As Petrov stayed in the room, he was surprised when the door opened and Prime Minister Winslet, along with the prime minister of Canada, stepped inside.

He knew why they walked in, or at least hoped he did. He felt a sense of relief when he saw their faces.

"Please don't think I'm abandoning your efforts," Winslet said. "I'm not. I am just trying to do what's best for my country."

Petrov nodded. "So am I." He shifted his eyes to the Canadian prime minister. "And you are here, why?

"This situation affects us very much." The Canadian prime minister said. "It is too close. We will do what we can to aid you and assist you in whatever endeavor you decide. But we ask that in exchange for our participation, you wait until our intel comes in."

"What intel would that be?" asked Petrov.

"We have people in there. But we cannot reach them. We are sending teams in to find out what is going on. To get an in-depth look."

"That I can agree to," said Petrov.

"May I ask," said Prime Minister Winslet, "while I realize the urgency of the situation, there seems to be a rush to get a decision. A good offense is planning. Is it because of the food shortage now?"

"It is not the food," Petrov answered strongly. "Do you not get it? At all? Yes, they are now controlling sixty percent of the world's food supply, that is troublesome. But more so, they are now in control of the second biggest nuclear arsenal in the world. I cannot have that. The world cannot have it. Can you?"

# CHAPTER ELEVEN

## Holly River Base, WV

It looked like the classic version of the old-school game Stratego. Little flags set up on a map. But instead of a generic landscape it was a topography map of the United States. It was spread out on a table, with Gus center of it all, Steve to his right, and a few military men joined.

"Right now, we know of nineteen camps," Gus said. "There are probably more but this is all we can confirm."

"Here's the problem," Troy said. "Once you hit any of them, the others are going to go on high alert."

"That's why we are going to have to hit as many as we can at the same time," Gus replied.

"Can we coordinate that?" Steve asked.

Gus nodded. "I believe we can. We don't need the manpower, it can be done quietly if done correctly."

"Infiltrate?" Troy asked. "Two, three people on the inside."

Gus moved his finger down to the map. "Exactly. Two or three on the inside, get us intel, get us in. If we do this at the right time, we only need a few good snipers to take out the guards, and the detainees can walk right out the door. That many people, they don't have enough soldiers to hold them back."

"Which begs an answer to the next question," Steve said. "What are we going to do with all these people. Here … Caldwell." He touched the map. "Thousands of people. Most of them displaced as it is, lost their homes, we open the fence, they walk out, then what? What are they going to do? To be honest, they're being fed and cared for in that prison. Freedom is a good incentive but so is living."

"The United States is huge," Gus said. "There are hundreds, maybe even thousands of small towns not even on the radar of the Procs. We get them there. Spread the word."

"We'd have to get the towns on board first," Steve said. "Find them. Secure them, before we even liberate the camps and lead the detainees there."

"Then what?" Troy asked. "We get them there. Then what? Convince them to fight with us?"

"I don't think that will be a worry," said Gus. "This country was under attack, their homes were destroyed, family members lost, dead. After all that and then being taken prisoner, I don't think they'll say, 'thank you' and walk away. I think they're gonna say to us, 'what do you need us to do?' They'll fight," Gus stated assuredly. "Once we get enough people that are over the shell shock and standing up for themselves, we're gonna see a whole different war unfold."

## Dallas, Texas

It was the seventh hospital General Liu had visited in just a few days. Dragging his aide around with him. He was grateful for the aide, Sergeant Huang. While Liu was quiet around him at first, Huang had not betrayed Liu or turned him in for veering from mission.

His mission went from a restructuring effort on paper, to a humanitarian one that wasn't acknowledged or allowed.

He, in a sense, had become a rebel

It wasn't that he didn't love his country or didn't want it to be victorious, he just wanted to play fair. Granted, war wasn't fair, but part of the thrill of victory was like in the game of chess, to champion your opponent through skill and strategy. If the current war was truly likened to the game of chess, then the United States entered the game missing several pieces including their queen. They were at a severe disadvantage. One China basked in.

It wasn't as if the general never thought of war with the United States, he had. In his ideal scenario, China had won the war over fear of might and disaster through financial ruin. Not fear of disease and disaster through stolen opportunities brought on by cowards who wished to overthrow their own government. When he thought back to that, to those men and women who planned to do their own liberation of their country, he wondered if they thought it through.

Sure, it was easy to bring a big man to his knees, but what if he did not stay down.

Liu believed the United States would not stay down, until he saw the sickness. It had spread faster than he imagined and it wasn't only Americans affected. He had received reports that Chinese soldiers and healthcare workers were lying in cots next to Americans.

And Fen Shu ... she had avoided him. She had not taken his calls nor was she ever at the meeting place. But he lucked out. While visiting Dallas, he had heard she was at a detention camp, and without announcing his arrival, General Liu sought out Fen.

"We are sure she is here?" Liu asked Huang.

"Yes, sir. My contact with her camp has said as much," Huang replied.

"You're a good man."

Liu meant those words. It was obvious to him that Huang was a seasoned veteran who had as much love for China as Liu did. Huang refrained from saying anything that could be considered treason, such as negative statements about the war. But Liu gauged how he felt. Huang was an ally and fast becoming the only friend he had in the foreign land.

"There," Huang said with appoint.

Liu rode front seat passenger in the jeep and Huang pointed to Fen just inside the fenced area speaking to soldiers. She wore a uniform and a gasmask over her face. He could still see her eyes and when he pulled up, they widened.

"Stay here. I wish you not to be part of this confrontation. For your own good."

Once the jeep had stopped, Liu stepped out and walked straight to Fen.

There was no avoiding him.

"Agent Shu, may I have a word?"

She nodded and followed him away from the earshot of others.

"I would request you remove that mask," he said.

"I prefer for my safety that I leave it on."

"Then you know about the illness."

"I do."

"Remove the mask. You are at a detainment camp."

"There is illness here. Our experts say it is airborne, highly contagious, remains alive for thirty-six hours in the air and on surfaces, and its current fatality rate without treatment is ninety-percent."

"What experts give you this information?" he asked. "I have been searching for it. I need to know what it is."

"It is a variation of EV-71. A manmade synthetic form of it."

"A biological weapon?" he asked.

"Yes."

"Would this be the same one tested in 1994 that killed over three hundred children in less than ten days?"

"It would be, yes," she said.

"Then this is ours. We did this."

Smugly, she replied, "We did. I told you that we needed them helpless. This is the way to do so."

"Our own men and woman are infected."

"They are casualties of war," she said.

"Where?" he asked. "Where was it released?"

"We took a page from American history and tainted blankets. Those blankets were passed out at relief stations and camps close to every area hit by the bombs."

General Liu closed his eyes and lowered his head. "It was not needed."

"More than you realize, it was."

"Then for my sake and information, I want everything you have on it. It is now an enemy and one cannot defeat an enemy without knowing it." He turned to walk away.

"It is not an enemy that needs defeated. We can defeat it," she said.

General Liu stopped walking and turned back around to face her. "There is a cure."

"A treatment but it must be given within a few days."

"Why have we not given it out?"

"In time. It's our price. They want to save lives, they must pay the price. That price tag is surrender."

He felt as if he wanted to scold her like a child. It took everything he had to hold back his hand from waving a finger at her.

"You say the treatment needs to be given in a few days. What happens if the surrender doesn't come for a while?"

"The virus will spread and it will keep on spreading."

"You'll help that along."

"I will. General," she huffed out, "my job was to devise a plan to get, maintain, and keep the United States of America and make it the Unified Territory of China. I am doing so. My plan will succeed."

"With biological warfare."

Fen shrugged. "Whatever it takes to break the country. Remember, bombs and firepower destroy not only living creatures but things that we need. Disease destroys our biggest threat and something we don't need."

"There is no honor in winning a war this way."

"Yes, but, all that will be forgotten in the face of victory."

"Who will forget? You? I will not. I must do what I can to help those with this sickness."

"General," she said, "I must remind you that you took an oath. Should you go against this, this is wartime, you will be tried for treason and executed."

General Liu listened to her threat, then, filled with anger and shame, turned and walked away.

## Hanlen, WV

"Cal." Louise said his name so softly, almost a whisper, her eyes still closed. "Cal," she called for him, swatting away the cloth as he wiped down her head.

"What?" he replied compassionately. "What is it?"

"Stop. You don't need to do that."

"Yes, I do."

She whispered his name once more and then she fell back to sleep.

That was the way she had been, waking, passing out, talking, then quiet. Cal believed she was close to maybe turning that bend of a recovery but thought perhaps Dr. Dan believed otherwise.

Moments earlier he had gone over to check on Louise. He did so quietly, said nothing and walked away.

He didn't change her empty IV bag or give her the medication for pain.

Cal supposed the doctor had a lot on his mind. It had gotten hectic. Twelve people had died the day before in that gym, and Cal helped carry those bodies out. Each day someone passed away or someone got better enough to leave or stand and help. It cleared some space in the gym. Cal took advantage of that. He confiscated a corner and moved Louise there, grabbing a of couple blankets and making a wall of privacy.

He couldn't move her far, she needed the constant medical treatment, but he wanted to give her some dignity.

"Hey," Jake said softly as he parted the blanket curtain and stepped into the sectioned area. "I'm back if you want to take a break."

"Yeah, thanks." Cal stood with a stretch of his arms. "I want to do my rounds."

Jake nodded and claimed the chair next to Louise.

"She wake up at all?" Jake asked.

"A little here and there. She bitched at me."

"That's a good sign."

"It is. How is it out there?" Cal asked.

"We went south and east, of course, got some supplies, didn't go too far."

"Did you see anymore of … of them?"

"The enemy soldiers?" Jake shook his head. "No. Still can't figure out why they were in that piss-ant town. Parkersburg is not a big metropolis."

"On their way to Washington, maybe?" Cal guessed.

"Washington's gone, so I can't figure out why they were there. But I haven't seen any more and this was the third time I went out in two days."

"I saw some new faces working out there this morning. Did you meet them?" Cal asked.

"Yeah, but I heard they were here from the beginning. Locals. They're the ones that brought all these people here. But … since they aren't finding any more to bring in and with no reports of the new thing."

"What new thing?"

"Guys on the truck were talking about some new bug that's spreading through the camps and towns. They're saying that's why we haven't gotten any of the Chinese doctors because they're busy out west."

"You're kidding me? Nuclear weapons, an invasion, and now this?" Cal shook his head. "What's the rest of the world like?"

"You know as much as I do."

"Yeah, you're right. I'm going to go talk to Dr. Dan before my rounds. He was pretty quiet the last time he came in here. Louise is overdue to change her IV and medication. I'll be back." Cal drew back the blanket and stepped out.

He spotted the doctor across the gym standing at a table, his hands moving about the air and head going back and forth scanning the table as if searching. Cal felt bad for him. He knew he was busy, he was the only doctor and he looked worn out, tired. He also looked about twenty years older than his age of thirty-five.

Cal cleared his throat when he approached him. "Excuse me, Dr. Dan."

Dan turned around. "Oh, hey there, Cal." He turned away again and looked at the items on the table.

"Everything alright?" Cal asked. "Can I help you find something?"

"No. No, thanks. I'm trying to assess what we have and it's not much."

"Jake said they got some stuff."

"They did. Not enough. Our best bet is Charleston, but you and I know that town is probably sieged. There's a few more volunteer fire stations and emergency garages, we may find some medicine but we need IVs, probably have to make them ourselves."

"Let me know, I'll help."

"I know you will. Thank you."

"Speaking of help ... you checked on Louise. You didn't change her bag. Give her the meds. I didn't wanna just grab one, but I can if you're busy. I can change it."

Dan didn't reply.

"Dan?"

Heavily, he sighed and turned around. "Cal, supplies are low."

"You said that."

"They're also a commodity. Louise ... she isn't good, Cal. She... she isn't going to get anymore medication."

"What?"

"I'm sorry."

"If you don't give her the meds, she will die."

"She probably will die anyhow. She isn't good. She didn't respond to the Prussian Blue. We'll give her saline to keep her hydrated, but that's it. I can't justify using the medication on her, I can't."

"So, we give up."

"I have to give up. If you want to try to take her up to Parkersburg or maybe Charleston. Our illustrious invaders have hospitals set up there."

"You think it's worth a shot?"

"You can try. But you have to be careful. There are new cases of that virus going around. There might be up there."

Cal nodded. He saw a woman and two men moving around the gym. They were the workers he noticed the day before. "Since you have help, I think I'll talk to Jake about going there."

"You do that, but Cal ..." Dan called out stopping Cal as he started to walk away. "I know this is painful and hard. But if ... if she survives it will be a long recovery and even then, she faces long-term debilitating effects. Allowing her to pass peacefully may be the humane thing to do."

Cal didn't reply, he only made eye contact with Dan and then walked back to the section where Louise rested.

"What's going on?" Jake asked.

Cal whispered, "He isn't giving her anymore meds. He says he can't justify it."

Jake nodded. "There are several others they stopped giving meds to as well."

"It's not fair," Cal said. "How can they do that?"

"Don't take this wrong," Jake said, "but put yourself in the other position. Say Louise had a good shot of getting better but needed more medication. Medication that was going to people who were going to die anyhow."

"We don't know that Louise is going to be one of those people."

"We know what her chances are."

Cal closed his eyes and shook his head in disgust.

"I'm not being a dick here, Cal. I'm just being honest."

"Cal," Louise called him weakly.

"Yes, I'm here." Cal rushed to her side.

Her eyes were open. "I'm in this room."

"What?" Cal asked.

"You're talking about me like ... like I ain't here. I am. I hear you."

"I'm sorry." Cal grabbed her hand. "I am so sorry. Look, we aren't staying. We aren't. We're leaving."

"Good," she said. "Good."

"I'm gonna take you out of here. Jake ... Jake if he will, can drive us."

"Absolutely."

"We're gonna shoot for Parkersburg or maybe even Charleston," Cal said. "Get you some medical attention there, see if they can—"

"No." Louise cut him off. "No. They're right. You can't waste medicine on me."

"We have to fight," Cal said. "We do. You said it was good we're leaving."

"Yes. Leaving this place. I want to leave. I ... want to go home. Ripley. We can't be far. I don't want to die here. I want to die at my home."

"You're not dying."

Louise closed her eyes tightly. "I wanna go home, Cal, please." She opened her eyes, looked at him, and squeezed his hand. "Please say you'll take me home."

"If he don't," a woman spoke up as she entered, "I will." A middle-aged woman with a hardened face, and a twang to her rough voice, stepped closer. "I'll take you home. I'm headed there. Ripley. I'll take ya."

"Excuse me," Cal said. "Who are you?"

"We met." She shook his hand. "You may not remember. I'm Helen. Helen Watson. Me, my son, and my husband tugged you off that boat."

"Oh, wow." Jake walked up to her and shook her hand. "Thank you very much."

Helen nodded. "I was coming back to check on her. I was speaking to that other fella, Rick?" She said his name as if she were guessing it. "He just got back from a run. I spoke to him. He's gonna stay back and help out here with my son. I'm headed down to Ripley, steal some of their volunteers for up here. The ones that can't help out … elsewhere."

Cal shook his head like a confused cat. "I … I'm lost. Ripley, her hometown, it has medical help?"

"About as much as here," Helen said. "Like here, it's

secluded, hasn't been touched or visited by the invasion. Right now, it's also a temporary hub. We have a better place, we'll go there. We're pulling resources and I am talking to every able-bodied person I can find. While you two aren't all that able bodied … yet. You will be. And your state right now, might work to our advantage. Especially you. You don't sound like you're from around here," she spoke to Cal.

"I'm not. I was on vacation."

"Oh, good," Helen said. "I spoke to the other guy. He doesn't look American, but he is. He's so damned Americanized he wouldn't pass for anything else. But you, Cal, you may be able to help."

Jake held up his hands. "I'm confused, and I am missing something. We volunteer here at this medical camp. I mean, I am happy to get Louise home, but they need us here."

"I'll get people for up here," she said. "People that can't do what we need them to do."

"And that is?" Jake asked.

"Fight," Helen answered, then glanced at Cal. "Infiltrate as an innocent bystander, not from this country. I can't get into details, mainly because I'll probably get them all wrong. We have a man in Ripley who can explain it all. We can get her home, comfortable, and get you to set up."

"So, you're starting a resistance?" Jake asked.

"Starting? Honey we have one. We're making it bigger," she said. "Don't know if you know this, but this country was attacked and invaded. We have a few hundred thousand Chinamen soldiers, screaming, 'we're here to save you,' when we know they're not. They not only came to our backyard and picked a fight, they took our country. And we"—she winked—"we're gonna take it back."

# CHAPTER TWELVE

## Swall, CA – San Joaquin Valley

They weren't kidding around.

At the crack of dawn the next day, just when Joe was having his breakfast, his workers showed up. The workers that were promised to him by the Asian man in a suit that came with the mayor.

All of the workers were young and fit, and they didn't say much. In fact, Joe swore they looked at him like he was some sort of prison warden.

They tossed out "Yes, sir," and "No, sir," like Joe was some kind of big shot.

He wasn't.

He never presented himself that way and his own workers treated him like a pal.

Where were his workers?

In fact, Joe didn't know a single person that showed up at his farm. They all arrived in the back of a truck, filed out, and waited.

Saul said he had the same experience. Only he called his workers, "Grown up Children of the Corn" people.

Joe explained what they had to do and only a few times did he have to stop and show them again. They were spot on, worked fast and moved toward the quota. A quota Joe thought was ridiculous.

He had to deliver six cartons of product a day. Six days a week. They gave him three days to get his first delivery in.

The workers produced well that first day, two cartons and Joe was impressed with that because they had not done so before.

When they were done for the day, they stood quietly, waiting on for the truck which arrived promptly at six o'clock.

Joe had a plan and he'd share it with the workers after they trusted him. He'd have them produce seven cartons a day, reaching their quota on Friday and when they came to work on Saturday they could just relax.

But like they didn't trust him, Joe was uncertain about them.

When the day arrived to deliver that first quota, they had already produced enough for the next day, but Joe didn't bring it. He figured if he showed up with more they'd raise the quota.

He wasn't even sure how he was supposed to turn it over. All he was told was take the daily quota to the distribution center.

*Where the heck is the distribution center?* Joe wondered. He figured worst came to worst he would head to the mayor's office.

Joe didn't like him.

The mayor was on his short list of people he was going to have a word with after the war was over and done.

On the morning the quota was due, Joe left the workers, loaded his truck, and headed into town.

The second he pulled into town, he felt as if it were surreal and his mind went immediately to the actor William H. Macy.

There was something about Macy that Joe just loved. He always judged celebrities on who he'd sit down and have a beer with, and Macy was one of them. The type of guy who would hang back on the porch, sipping a cold one, and enjoying Fat Joe's tomato salad.

He hadn't thought about Macy until he arrived into town.

Swall was a pretty little town, one of those places that could be on a postcard and a tourist attraction, had it not been so deep in the state of California. It was a town of farmers and Joe was one of them.

They knew him at the post office when he dropped off his crates and at the Print and Go where there was a UPS counter.

But it wasn't freaky.

Until that day, and Joe thought he stepped out of his truck into the movie *Pleasantville*. That's what made him think of Macy. He half expected everything to turn black and white. Had it been that town in that movie, it would have made sense. The streets were busier than he'd ever seen them. People were dressed in their Sunday best as they walked the streets, waving to each other and smiling.

Women with baby strollers moved up and down the sidewalks, the ice-cream man was dishing scoops from his cart for a nickel.

What year was it? Was Joe dreaming? The old playground center of town, the one that had rusted out years before and was always overgrown, was now painted brightly. The grass was cut while six children swung happily. Did they even have six kids in town?

He pulled up to the post office, figuring they'd know where the distribution center was. But they were closed. A Chinese solider was posted out front.

"Hey, Joe!" someone called out to him.

Joe turned around. It was Sam, he worked at the post office.

"We're closed."

"I see that."

"We'll be open soon. Don't you worry." Sam winked.

"I'm not. Right now, I need to know where this distribution center is."

"Oh, do you have to get your rations?"

"No, I'm fine."

"You should take your rations," Sam said. "Everyone does. Sign up and take them, Joe. It's at the old Ren Theater. Just ask for sign up."

"Okay, well, yeah, maybe I will." Joe glanced at him suspiciously cross-eyed. "I'll head on over, I have to drop off."

"Thank you, Joe."

"Hey, Sam, what the heck is going on around here? I mean, everyone is walking around happy-go-lucky."

"It's good to be alive, Joe."

"Yeah. So why dress up?"

"It's the rules. If you are out and about in town and not working you must be dressed in suitable clothing."

"Oh, who the hell made that rule?" Joe asked.

"It's a good rule, Joe. Gives people a sense of worth." He nodded at the Chinese solider. "It's a good rule."

Joe looked over his shoulder at the soldier. "It sucks you know, that rule. Just saying. Okay, I'm headed over." Joe headed toward his truck.

"Say, Joe?" Sam called out. "We started a pierogi club at the church. We're making them tonight. Would you like to join us?"

"A pierogi club?"

"Yeah, you know the pockets of dough with filling."

"I know what a pierogi is."

"Funny thing … everyone thought the Chinese invented them."

Joe grumbled to himself.

"But that's simply not true, no disrespect to our foreign guests here, they were just trying to take credit. The Polish people were like … nope, we got this. Got to love a pierogi, it's like a surprise every time you open one."

"Not really, Sam, if they're potato and cheese then you get potato and cheese."

"You should come, Joe."

"No, I'll pass but thanks." He headed toward his truck.

"You'll like these pierogi."

"I'm sure, but I'll pass. Thanks." Joe opened his door and climbed in his truck and whistled. Sam must have been stressed, he was really unlike himself.

It wasn't far to the theater and had Joe just driven around town he would have realized it was the place. People lined up before a table, while armed soldiers stood on guard.

Joe really wasn't in the mood to stand in line, then he noticed the 'deliveries' table and he loaded up the dolly with the first four cartons, took them over and headed back to the truck. When he returned with the last two Mary Lou Martin was seated at the table. She wore a wide smile and blue floral dress. Her husband ran one of the best fruit farms in the county.

"Hey, Joe, I have you dropping off," she said brightly, handing him a clipboard. "Just need you to sign. How are you doing?"

"Good. Thank you. You?"

"Wonderful. Just wonderful."

"That's good to hear." He handed back to the clipboard. "How does the payment work?"

"Not real sure, I know that it is monthly."

"Were you and Greg given a quota too?" Joe asked.

Mary Lou shifted her eyes to the soldier to the left. "No, we don't have a quota. I'm not … we're not doing the farming thing. These wonderful people took it over after Greg's passing."

"Say what? Passing? My God, Mary Lou. I am so sorry to hear that. I thought he was healthy as a horse?"

"He was. It was an accident. A skirmish and he was caught up in it."

Joe was truly shocked to hear the news. "When did he pass?"

"Four days ago."

"Four days."

"I'm good though, Joe. Life is good. I don't have the farm to worry about, I have this job and I have pierogi club at the church. You should join us, Joe. You really need to join us."

"Maybe another day," Joe said. "I have to head back. Got the zoning committee at my place."

"Zoning committee?" she asked.

"That's what I call my new workers, because they're all zoned out. See you around and I am really sorry about Greg."

"No problem! Oh, hey, Joe, how's Tobias?"

Joe stopped cold and a lump formed in his chest. "I don't know. He was doing that road trip thing and I ... I haven't heard from him since everything happened."

"You know there's a database. It's made up of health camps, refugee centers, displaced survivors. It's updated constantly. Every morning you can check to see if a loved one is on there. It's only open until ten, you just missed it."

"Really? Where at?"

"The library."

"Thank you, Mary Lou. I will come back. Thank you for that."

"Sure thing, and Joe, you'll find him."

Joe stopped walking and nodded his gratitude. "I'm sure wherever my nephew is, he's standing on his feet."


## Cleveland, OH


The butt of the rifle landed square on Toby's face and he knew before he even hit the ground that his nose was broken.

He fell back in what felt like slow motion. He could hear Harris yelling, but Toby was in so much pain, it was muffled.

He landed hard to the ground with a crack to his back. However, he was resilient. As if he weren't even hurt, he rolled to his side to get back up. Only making it to his knees, Toby was tromped by a soldier and smashed face first into the concrete.

All because Toby, innocently enough, protested when he saw one of the soldiers grab Marissa inappropriately and then put her in the back where the women were gathered.

"Hey, dude, what the hell?" Toby said reaching for the soldier's hand. At that point he was shoved back, and when they did that, he fell from the truck.

"Toby, run," Harris told him.

But before he could do anything, just as he got to his feet, the soldier pummeled him with that rifle. How he kept consciousness, Toby didn't know. Even though it was fuzzy to him.

When they lifted him from the ground, they did so holding under his arms and dragged him face down. He watched his own blood pour from him.

They tossed him less than gently back into the rear of the truck. He rolled when the vehicle jolted and started to move.

Harris reached down and helped him up to the bench. "You alright?"

Toby didn't know how to answer that. Of course, he wasn't

alright. A man across from him took off his over shirt and handed it to Toby for his bleeding.

He was grateful and held it to his nose. It was all new to Toby, he had never been in a physical confrontation his life, yet there he was with a bleeding nose and a bruised ego. Worse than that he was confused, he just didn't understand what was going on. He didn't know where they were taking them or why. But he didn't need to have the answers to those questions to know that wherever he was heading … it wasn't good.

## Ripley, WV

There were many hand paintings ranging from abstract to realism, so many in fact they filled the entire front sun room of the single-story frame house.

Louise's house.

She put out that she handled the trip just fine, but Cal knew better. Each bump, each stop, she bit her bottom lip, closing her eyes as if trying to hide the pain.

She was in pain and had no medication to help it.

Helen went to get something while Cal settled her into the house.

"Where will you feel most comfortable?" Cal asked. "Can I help you to bed?"

"No." Louise smiled with a gentleness. "Help me into the easy chair by the window. Always was my favorite place to sit."

It was a small front room or living room with a couch, television, and a beat-up tan reclining chair. He walked her to it, swiveled the chair to face the window and Louise plopped in it. She reached for the handle but struggled to even move it.

"Relax," Cal told her, then gently reclined the chair.

"There's a blue afghan on the sofa, can you get that for me?"

"Sure." Cal took a few steps back and grabbed the folded blanket that was over the back of the couch. He brought it to Louise, flapped it out, and covered her.

"Ah." She pressed her lips together and forced a smile. "This is nice."

"Can I get you anything?" Cal asked.

"No, I'm good. This is nice. This is so much better." Her head turned to the knock at the door.

Cal peeked out the window and saw it was Helen. He hollered out a, "Come in."

A few seconds later, Helen entered the living room. "I got you a lollipop," she said, holding up a tiny narrow packet.

"A what?" Cal asked.

"They call them lollipops." She opened the package, pulling out a cotton swab looking item with a tiny vial attached to the end. "It's fentanyl. Put this in your mouth like a lollipop." She gave it to Louise. "It will take away the pain."

"Where did you get that?" Cal asked.

"I went to the clinic. Those are used in the field for injured soldiers. That should help her rest while we go to our meeting.

Cal nodded and looked at Louise. He placed his hand over hers. "Hey, I'll be right back. Okay?"

"You do what you need to do," Louise told him. "Take your time. I'm not going anywhere."

Cal smiled at her, leaned down and placed his lips to her forehead. "I'll be right back. Enjoy your lollipop."

He stepped away, taking another look before leaving the living room. A part of him felt guilty for leaving her, but she seemed fine and at peace being in her own home.

Cal's meeting wouldn't take long, at least that was what Helen said. Louise's medication would kick in soon. Cal was certain she'd pass out and he would return before she even woke enough to realize what had happened.


He wasn't what Cal expected to see. On the way to meet him, Helen said he was a military man who was protecting the president at the onset of the war. Cal expected someone staunch and fully decorated. Instead he saw a man in blue jeans and a T-shirt who balked when Cal called him captain.

"Troy," he corrected. "Please. Not that I don't serve my

country, it's just not safe to be in uniform right now. Please, have a seat."

Cal pulled out a chair at the two-seater table in the empty café closed to the public. No sooner did he sit down, Troy tossed a passport on the table. It had seen better days and Cal looked curiously at it.

"Open it," Troy said.

Cal flipped it open, it was his. "How ..."

"It was in a bag on the boat. Helen brought that to Steve, we've been waiting for you to get well. See, we can get an American to act as if they are from another country, but this ... this proves you are."

"What do you need from me? I'm not soldier."

"What do you ... *did* you do for a living back home?"

"Basically projects, buildings, concrete."

"Construction?"

"I was a project manager."

Troy nodded. "Can you pull off saying you're an architect?"

Cal laughed. "Why would I say that?"

"Because we need someone they are going to trust and right now, our other inside person says they are looking for someone to design and build, change a small town in Ohio into pretty much a fortified internment camp."

Cal lifted his hand and let it drop to the table. "I don't understand what you need."

"There is a small town south of Cleveland. Right now, they have about eight thousand detainees there. We want to liberate that camp. In order to do so, we need someone on the inside who can help us do that."

"You already have someone on the inside," Cal said.

"Not trusted. He's American. You are not. They are having job recruitments just outside of there. You go under the guise you want to go back home and that you'll help out where needed. You have the passport to prove you aren't from here. You have no obligations to this country."

Cal sat back with an exhale. "How am I supposed to communicate with you?"

"Our person on the inside will be in touch. There are more details. He has a military direct phone, he sends us messages. I'm not going to say more until you give your agreement."

"Why, Captain, would I want to help?"

Troy hesitated before answering. "Everything that happens here affects your country. It already has. The UK is in chaos, it's only a matter of time before World War Three breaks out and we don't want that. We get this country back, we take it back, we may avoid global catastrophe."

"How do you know my country is in chaos?"

"We were in communication before our outpost was hit. Will you do it? Will you help us?"

Cal looked down to his folded hands and raised his eyes. "Can I have tonight to think about it? I need to check with a friend who is ill."

Troy nodded. "Yes. I'll be here until tomorrow. Helen can take you back now."

Cal stood and extended his hand to Troy. "I'll let you know my decision shortly, I promise."

"Thank you."

Cal stepped back, paused, reached down, and grabbed his passport. He placed it in his pocket and turned to leave. What was being asked of him wasn't some minor thing. It was a big undertaking, serious spy stuff and wasn't a one shot, one day deal.

It was dangerous.

He had Louise to think about and that was priority. Not that Cal didn't want to help, but if he was going to be honest, he wasn't sure he wanted to put his life on a line for a country he wasn't that vested in.

<><><><>

Helen drove Cal back to Louise's little house. Turning the bend, he caught a glimpse of her in the window.

"They really need you," Helen said as she stopped the truck. "We need you."

"I understand that," Cal replied. "Is it going to make a difference? You said there are hundreds of thousands of Chinese soldiers. Can we defeat them?"

"There are still two hundred million Americans. Yes, we can."

"I will think about it." Cal opened the door and stepped out. He walked to the house imagining what Louise would say. She'd be for it. If she were well enough, she would take up arms and fight. That was who she was. Fiery and full of life.

He knocked once on the main door to announce his arrival and stepped in. "Louise," he called out, walking in.

After closing the door, he took in the silence.

"Hey," he said walking into the living room. "I met with them. They want me to go in there and try to get information. I know what you'll say, but I hate to leave you." He stepped to the chair. "Look they had my passport and ..." He paused. "Shit. You're sleeping."

Louise had her head propped on her hand and tilted to the side.

"I'm sorry." He lowered his voice then grabbed for the blanket that had fallen a little from her. The moment he lifted it ... he froze.

Louise wasn't sleeping.

She had passed away some time while he was gone, in that short span of time.

Cal's heart sank to the pit of his stomach as he dropped to his knees at her chair side. How did it happen? She had been such a big part of his life, through such a huge ordeal, yet, she slipped quietly away after her body had taken such a beating from the radiation poisoning. He felt horrible he wasn't there. Not there to hold her, say goodbye or even his feelings. He placed his hand over her wrist, lowered his head to her arm, and stayed there. He just couldn't move.

# CHAPTER THIRTEEN

## Holly River Base, WV

"Glad you made it back before sundown," Gus said to Troy. He was seated on the front porch of Bear's house, sipping a cup of coffee relaxing, when he saw Troy pull up in the pick-up truck and step up.

"I still have a few hours before dark."

"Any trouble?" Gus asked.

"Nothing. No Procs. I took the back ways. What are you doing here?" Troy asked

"Thought I would take a long shift here to monitor the radio, and any other coded transmissions that come in. Plus, I want to double-check all the Morse code that has come in so far," Gus said. "That was kind of my specialty for a while."

"You know we have the decoder, right?"

"Yep. But, I'm old-school. Don't trust those things. I'd rather give it a once over myself."

"Makes sense."

"So, any word?" Gus asked.

"You mean about the Englishman?" Troy shook his head. "No. I got the feeling from him that it wasn't his fight."

"But it is his flight. Did you tell him that?"

"I did. But it is up to him. When I left them, Helen was riding him back. She was going to get him all the details. Hopefully we'll find out soon what he does. He knows where to find the means of communication and how to locate our inside guy. That's all we could do, the rest is up to him."

Gus nodded. "Thank you for trying. I just know that we have to do something and we have got to get it done soon. We have the diversions in place that we want to execute before we start camp liberation."

"When will the diversion hits begin?"

"Few days. I'm worried. There's another whole line of fleet coming over across the Pacific. It's not gonna be long before they hit us with another invasion. If that happens, I don't know where we will stand on this," Gus said.

"I wonder why they haven't hit us again yet."

"My guess, they're waiting for the official surrender. Since they have the president."

"Surrender?"

"Yeah, you spent a little time with her. What do you think?

Do you think she will surrender? If she does, then it's done."

"I don't know." Troy shrugged and shook his head. "She's hard to read. She really is. She wants to do well, but she's in over her head."

"Hopefully, she'll hold off enough for us to get this rolling."

"Gus, really, I understand what we are doing. And I am a part one hundred percent. But ..." Troy said. "How are we going to do this? There's not that many of us. How are we going to pull this off when we're on our own?"

"My friend," Gus said, "how do you think I got the information? We are far from being on our own."

## USNORTHCOM, Colorado Springs, CO

General Welch was in the right place at the right time. He wasn't supposed to be in Colorado, but when another member of the Joint Chiefs of Staff took ill, he filled in for the war games exercise at the Cheyenne Mountain Military base. He was there when everything went down

When word arrived that there was a domestic terror attack taking place, the first thing he did was seal the base. It was NORAD and the USNORTHCOM, the end-all-be-all, top-dog military installation. Then as he dismissed it as something they could handle, things turned and he received intel that perhaps a foreign entity was also involved. When that occurred, whether it was true or not, the first order of business, after the base, was to move ships and subs. The biggest line of defense for the United States was stationed outside of Bangor, Washington, and General Welch made sure they were in a position to defend their country.

He'd listened and was impressed as Lieutenant Colonel Gilbert in Alaska successfully intercepted as many incoming missiles as they could, then Welch ordered Gilbert to seal his base as well.

Typically, the base would have emptied out roughly a hundred people, but the domestic hit came just before the end of the work day and Cheyenne Mountain had over three hundred people inside.

It was command central for missile control with blast doors that were made to withstand a nuclear explosion. That never came, but the invasion did.

Outside of Cheyenne was a war zone.

Soldiers took up arms and the battle was continuous. The Chinese invaders wanted in. There was a report that as many as seven thousand Chinese soldiers were trying to break the doors. They blasted them constantly.

The mountain was the flag and Welch's job was to protect that flag at all cost.

Ammunition was running low, and while confidence was high they couldn't get in, Welch still worried. However, from inside he did what any good military leader would do, he prepared for the war and charted a plan. He was in constant contact with many resistance outlets.

Eventually, he believed they would flip the switch, and that wasn't far off. A long-time soldier, Welch knew there were mistakes made by the Chinese in their quest to take over America. Mistakes he would use to his advantage.

Their invasion against America was badly planned.

Paul Regal was a journalist assigned to cover the war games military exercise. He wasn't seasoned so when everything occurred, Paul panicked and stayed close to the general. He asked a million questions, not for a story, but to be informed.

Within days, however, he was becoming an expert.

The general kept him informed and Paul helped the general, almost as an assistant.

"Where are they now?" the general asked a specialist who manned the control panel.

"In position, sir."

"Tell them to keep moving, we don't need them picked up. We want them ready though." Welch turned and faced Paul. "I got them where I want them, I can't do anything yet. Diversion, liberation has to occur first."

"What about what's happening with the enemy outside?" Paul asked.

"That's annoying. We need them out of the way to get our men and planes out there." The general huffed. "Almost like a stand still. Wish to God, I could just utilize the nine. But all in due time."

"The nine?" Paul asked.

"My esteem fleet. Do you know what the great thing about Ohio-class subs is?"

Instead of Paul, the specialist answered. "Anyone that read a Tom Clancy novel knows what is special about them."

"True." The general chuckled.

"I don't," Paul said. "What's so special?"

"They are the most destructive force created by humankind. Each of those subs carries twenty-four Trident II submarine-launched ballistic missiles that can be fired under water and reach a target seven thousand miles away. When a missile enters the atmosphere, it's firing in at Mach 24 and splits into eight different missiles. Son, we're talking a hundred and ninety missiles per sub; can wipe out a couple dozen Chinese cities in an instant. We got nine of them subs out there, waiting and ready to go."

"Jesus," Paul said. "What happens when you fire them? What will the Chinese do?"

"Nothing." Welch nodded. "They have most of their forces out at sea and here. Who's watching the farm, right? They don't have the fire power to intercept or retaliate. Nor would they send anything over here with their payload digging in. It's all about the grain, we got the grain here, they won't destroy what's left. However, they may not have the payload, but we do. That's why they need to take this base so badly."

"So, you're going to hit them hard here then hit them hard there?" Paul asked.

"That's the plan. But our hands are tied. We need to get out there and off this base. I'm just waiting right now for word that we all gonna clear the field."

"Sir," the specialist called out, holding a phone. "I got him. It's a secure line."

Hurriedly, Welch snatched the phone. "Mr. President," he said. "This is General Welch. Com Headquarters. Yes, sir. Tell me you're going to bring a little vodka to the party." Welch clenched his fist and smiled. "Yes, sir, thank you. We will be in touch." He handed the phone to the specialist. "Tell our men outside to pull in. Those who remain out there, mask up." His eyes went to the map. "In one hour this shit outside is going to end."

## Swall, CA – San Joaquin Valley

The zoning committee, as Joe called them, were all working at a steady and freakishly unison pace. He needed a general foreman, someone he could say to, "Hey, I'll be right back." But he didn't think any of them would even notice if he did leave.

Joe wanted to check on Saul, see how he was doing with his workers and he wanted to tell him about Greg. A part of Joe wondered what the death by skirmish meant. Maybe he'd get a chance to talk to Mary Lou without the presence of soldiers. He blamed that on her odd behavior, but what of his workers? If Joe didn't know better, he would have sworn they were all brainwashed.

He didn't know if it was his workers or all farm workers, and that was another reason he made his way to Saul's.

He tried at first reaching him by phone but there was no answer. When he arrived at Saul's he could see the workers in the field, only specks of them as they moved, bent over picking the berries.

After parking directly in front of Saul's Joe honked the horn, stepped from the truck, and honked again.

"Hey, Saul?"

Saul appeared at the screen porch door. He didn't step out, staying inside and was shadowed. "Come on in."

Saul left the door and Joe walked up to the porch and in.

"I saw your workers out there," Joe said as he walked in. "How they doing you?"

"Good," Saul's voice came from the kitchen. He then coughed.

"Don't know about yours, but mine are like robots."

"Mine, too." Saul coughed again.

"So, I went to town to drop off my quota." Joe walked to the kitchen. "Everyone is all dazzled up in their Sunday best. Seems it's a new rule …"

Saul stood at the stove, back toward Joe. He coughed about three or four times in a row.

"You okay?"

"Yeah, got some sort of bug. Go on."

"Anyhow, I saw Mary Lou Martin. Perky as a peacock and Greg died four days ago."

"Yeah, I heard."

"She said there was a skirmish."

"Skirmish hell," Saul said. "He wanted them off his farm and they shot him."

"Goddamn it, was it worth it?"

"To him it was." Saul fixed a cup and turned around.

"Jesus!" Joe said in shock. "You *are* sick."

Saul's face was pale, his eyes dark, and he had raw looking sores around his mouth and nose.

"I feel like crap."

"You look it. Is that the herpes on your mouth?"

"No!" Saul barked and walked toward the table. "It's cold sores. They started last night. Hurt like a bitch." He paused to cough. "Got them on my hands, too. Did you want tea?"

"No. If I did I'd fix it myself. You ought to get to bed and rest."

"I will as soon as my workers load on the bus. Might need you to take my quota if I don't feel better tomorrow."

Joe nodded. "I can do that. But maybe you should see a doctor."

"I will in a couple days. Just want to avoid town." Saul took a sip of his tea. "I didn't want to miss the pierogi club tonight."

"Say what?" Joe asked, shocked. "You too? What in the world? Is it just a wartime social thing or are you really in the mood for pierogi? 'Cause I have a box of …"

"No, Joe." Saul shook his head with a smile, paused, cringed, and touched his sores.

"Is there something more to this? If there is, it's an open invitation to the firing squad."

"I honestly don't know. But … Go, okay? At the very least there'll be homemade pierogi."

Joe, gripping the back of a chair, merely grumbled an indecisive 'hmm.'

<><><><>

Against his better judgement, Joe put on a nice button-down shirt, following the dress code in town since he was giving in and hitting the pierogi club. For Saul's sake. Saul said he had to contribute an ingredient and Joe didn't know what he would contribute. He figured shortening was a sure bet. He opened the pantry for his contribution and saw the apron hanging there. Figuring 'what the heck' he brought that too, just in case there was a cooking dress code as well.

It was in the basement of St. Mathew's Church, the same place they held the monthly bizarre and bake sale. The place of the fish fry's and occasional spaghetti dinner.

There were at least a dozen cars in the church lot. Joe parked his truck and walked around to the side of the building to use the exterior stairwell to get below.

He had some ideas or possibly fantasies about what the pierogi club was all about, until he saw the Chinese soldier posted outside the door.

"Evening," Joe said with a nod.

The soldier didn't reply he just checked the items in Joe's hand and lifted his eyes judgmentally over the apron.

"Don't judge," Joe said, "the color works for me." He pushed the door open and walked inside.

The basement was a decent size and set up with a small entrance way and coat check in just before the hall. The kitchen was in the back.

He pushed through the entry swinging doors and stepped into the hall. There was a hum of soft voices, and then he saw the group of people, about twenty, standing around two tables joined width wise, and they were making dough.

By them, standing close was another armed Chinese soldier.

"Joe!" Mary Lou called out. "You made it!"

"I did." Joe walked over to the table. "I'm filling in for Saul. He's in the mood for pierogi." Joe placed the can of shortening on the table. "I brought my contribution."

Mary Lou smiled and lifted the lid. Her eyes reflected disappointment as she lifted the lid. "It's … it's shortening."

"Yep, that's what it says on the can."

"Oh." She placed it down. "Wash your hands, grab some gloves, we'll make dough."

"You know, I have to tell you," Joe said, "I was wondering how you guys were able to have a pierogi club. I mean, I was worried they'd see this as an unlawful gathering, especially with the uh …" He looked at the soldier. "Take over and all."

The soldier lifted his hand and waved it a little as he smirked. "Oh, no, dude, I'm good. You're cool."

When he spoke with no dialect, sounding like a pure southern Californian surfer guy, Joe nearly lost his balance.

Mary Lou whispered, "It's Staff Sergeant Eddie Edmunds.

166

Isn't it brilliant? Bruce here recognized him right away." She nodded to another man.

"Was his gym teacher all through elementary school," Bruce said.

"How the heck do they not know?" Joe asked.

"I speak the language fluently," Edmunds replied. "My dialect is sometimes off, so I keep what I say short and sweet. They don't know. Everyone thinks I came from another unit. There are so many of these guys. It was easy to do."

"Are there any more United States soldiers doing double agent duty?" Joe asked.

"Several, yes," Edmunds said.

Joe looked down to the table. "This isn't a pierogi club?"

"Oh, we make pierogi," Mary Lou said. "It's our feint. Edmunds covers, we find out everything from him. We produce pierogi, but we're something more. This is a pocket of resistance."

"Each pocket, in each town that has a takeover is meeting like this," Bruce said softly. "It will be a coordinated plan, each town doing their part. Right now, Swall and this valley have about three thousand soldiers. Each set up in groups, battalions, so when you look at it, it's not many, making it easy to do."

"Not many making what easy to do?" Joe asked.

Bruce hesitated before answering, "To take out."

Trying to speak quietly, Joe in shock squeaked out, "What?

You mean …" His eye shifted and he paused when he saw a man working with dough. "Hey, wait a second … you work for me."

The man nodded. "I do. My name is Josh."

"What the hell is up with your guys? You act like zombies."

"We have to. Each of us has a family member at a detention camp and they are holding that over our heads," Josh answered.

"There is a sequence of events," Mary Lou said. "All coordinated to let them know we mean business. If this works, we can take this country back. But everyone has to do their part, Joe. Everyone. You want your country back you have to do what it takes. And you are more vital than you think."

"No." Joe shook his head.

"Yes," Mary Lou said. "They are storing your tomatoes, at the end of the week, those crates of tomatoes are going …"

Joe covered his ears and shook his head. "No. You hear me," he whispered harshly. "No. I will not be a part."

"What happened?" Mary Lou asked. "When you lost that weight did you lose your balls? Everyone said it. Fat Joe is gone. Yeah, he is. The Joe Garbino I knew stood up for what was right. He wasn't scared, he fought. Fat Joe wouldn't sit idly by doing what he was told. He probably would have been shot like Greg. But that Joe is gone."

Joe grumbled. "He is not gone and my balls are just fine, thank you."

"The only way we can do this is if everyone does their part."

"There are so many of them."

"But there are even more Americans," Mary Lou said. "Think about it, Joe. Think about it. In the meantime, stick around, it will look suspicious if you leave. And ..." She handed him the apron. "Make some pierogi."

# CHAPTER FOURTEEN

## Fourteen Days Post Bombs

## Caldwell, OH

*"I'll be there,"* Cal said. *"I'm part of it."*

Cal walked a good distance, it was better that way.

*"Caldwell, Ohio has only five roads that go into it,"* Troy told him. *"Each one is sealed, blocked off."*

Walking along Highway 77, Cal had seen the Caldwell sign earlier and knew he was close. He just didn't know what would happen.

*"They will ask you a lot of questions. Get in the state of mind you want to go home and will do whatever it takes,"* Troy said. *"Across the highway is a correctional institute. Rumor has it they killed all inmates and are using the property now as holding. We don't know. Whatever the case, we want those people especially."*

*"You want criminals to fight for you?"*

*"We want people."*

Before Cal even arrived at Caldwell, he saw the road block. Cars were lined up leading to it. All of them were empty and abandoned. At the end of the line of cars was a fence and he could make out several large military vehicles.

*"Our inside man is not in a position of trust, he will reach out to you, he will give you the means to communicate."*

*"How will I know him?"*

*"He'll come to you. You know what we need."*

Cal couldn't believe he'd agreed to do it, but what else did he have to do? Louise would have wanted him to and probably would have scolded him if he refused.

His instructions swirled in his mind, he was given so much direction and so little time.

He was tired. He was far from a hundred percent and hoped to rest but knew that was impossible. He heard it about the same time he saw it.

Weapons being engaged, and words shouted out to him in a language he didn't understand.

Cal had arrived at the check point and did the only thing he could. He raised his arms in surrender.

"I just want to go home, can you guys help me get home and out of this Godforsaken place?" Cal tried to convey to the soldiers but was treated like a wanted fugitive.

He was roughly pulled aside, his items taken and searched. He was patted down for weapons, but they did take interest when they discovered his passport.

They returned his backpack and walked him through the security fence. A block into the walk on the right was a gas station, one of those convenience store types. There was a gas tanker there and it looked as if they were taking the gas.

Cal took in everything, just as asked. The entrance off of Highway 77 was barely guarded, he guessed that was because of the sea of cars parked across all six lanes of the road.

Soldiers mulled around, and there didn't appear to be any civilians. Clearly, that area was for military only.

After passing the gas station, Cal was brought into a large box-style tent. Inside, decorated military personnel spoke to each other and gathered around a large table. They paid no mind to his presence. The soldier that escorted Cal inside held up his hand to Cal, signaling for him to stay put.

Cal stopped walking and watched the soldier walk over to one of the leaders. He presented the leader with Cal's passport, then the gentleman nodded and walked toward Cal.

He held out his hand to a table and chairs and Cal sat.

Cal wasn't familiar with Chinese army rank but could guess by the stack of upside down Vs on the patch on his arm, the man was a sergeant.

The sergeant spoke slowly and with pronounced and slightly broken English.

"You are in America. Why?"

"Vacation," Cal replied. "I want to go home."

"I see. Home. London?" he asked.

"Yes. Is that possible? Is there a way for you to help me get home? I'll do what I need to do until then."

"I will make some calls," he said, lifting the passport. "I will need to hold on to this."

"Yes. Absolutely."

"Mister … Calhoun, is it?"

Cal nodded.

"It could be some time. You would be willing to work the camp as an ambassador? We need English-speaking workers."

"Yes, I will."

"You do not look healthy."

Cal shook his head. "I have been sick. Radiation."

"We will see about getting you a job and bed, until then let us get you medical treatment. Follow me." He walked by Cal and out of the tent. Cal followed.

He didn't know what the job and bed would entail, but he did know one thing, he was in and that was reason for his being there.

## USNORTHCOM, Colorado Springs, CO

Welch had to wait twenty-four hours before he could leave the mountain and investigate.

The raging battle, continuous gunfire over what Welch called 'the flag' had ended. One call out, and the rescue came in the form of an experimental bomb from Russia.

It was so different that even masks didn't work. Welch lost three men. Men who believed they were safer and stayed outside to keep firing.

The bomb was not an explosion, it didn't contain fire power, radiation, or some biological agent. Instead, when the bomb detonated it spewed trillions of what Welch could only describe as microscopic shards of glass or similar to glass.

If any landed on the skin, they were absorbed and like acid ate their way through the layers of epithelia. But their main route of attack was inhalation and that caused an agonizing death.

The microscopic shards entered the person's airways, embedding in the lining of the bronchial tube and lungs. Every breath taken thereafter, pushed the shards deep into the tissue, cutting it to shreds.

The victim coughed and choked as the entire respiratory system was annihilated, the lining of the lungs turned into a slosh and they drowned in their own blood.

It was horrendous and painful.

It was … inhumane, but the only way to bring a halt to the situation outside of Cheyenne Mountain. He supposed another wave would come, and he was confident that they wouldn't detonate a nuclear weapon, at least not yet. Not when they needed access to the United States Arsenal. It was the only control hub left. Welch made sure of it.

Until that time came when they'd retreat inside after another attack, Welch made his way outside to assess.

Twenty-four hours after they had wiped out the thousands of Chinese soldiers, no retaliation had occurred. No one from the Procs showed up. That told Welch they weren't in constant contact. The invasion was too big, there weren't enough hands on the battles to manage it properly. Things … soldiers … battalions slipped through the cracks. As did those who lost their lives at the massacre at Cheyenne.

Outside, General Welch wore covering over his entire body as a safeguard. The fence outside the compound was down, not that it did much anyway. The main tunnel entrance had been battered, and starting from the second he walked outside, Welch saw bodies.

They didn't just drop where they were. They died in various positions, holding onto their throats, bent over with piles of dried blood by them. Some were curled up and others even appeared as if they were crawling. Fingers scraping the ground, mouths wide open, probably screaming in agony.

Thousands of bodies scattered about.

It was quiet, and the battle had been won.

Welch wanted to feel bad, but he couldn't. Those thousands of lives lost paled in comparison to the millions of Americans who were now dead because of them.

The massacre at Cheyenne was not only the end of one page, but it was something else. Something bigger.

It was the opening of the starting gate.

General Welch put out word that it was time.

A call to arms to those ready to fight, the rise of the resistance and the beginning of what would be the biggest war America would ever face … Operation Recover Home.

# CHAPTER FIFTEEN

## Sixteen Days Post Bombs

## Mitton, TX

Perfect.

Fen couldn't ask for more perfection. It was exactly what they needed. The small town of Mitton was clean and picturesque. The townspeople moved about happily as instructed and there wasn't a single case of sickness.

Fen directed everything like a movie producer, knew what went where and how it should look.

Four photographers and videographers were present and she pointed to where and what they would photograph. An Asian news correspondent stood by, preparing for a broadcast.

"Play with the children," Fen instructed a group of soldiers. "Smile, laugh."

She pointed to the camera people to capture the group of people having coffee at an outdoor café, and those who laughed while in line to get provisions.

It was a beautiful sunny day, the best kind for a broadcast.

Fen grabbed another photographer and took him toward the distribution center set up as a market. She then instructed the news woman that the market would be a great backdrop, especially with the coffee shop right next door to it.

A little boy, no older than eight darted by, bumping into Fen. She stopped him.

He wore the brightest blue and green stiped shirt, his brown hair was messy, and his dimpled smile was adorable as he peered up to her.

"I brought the soldiers cakes," he said. "Our thank you for saving us."

Fen smiled at him. "Go on," she said. "They will like it."

She wanted to get the boy on video but he was too dirty. Perhaps she would find him, clean him, and then get him on camera. She reflected as she watched him carry the basket to the soldiers. He reminded her of her brother.

Her biological brother.

Always moving fast.

Fen wasn't born into a privileged life. In fact, she was very poor. They lived in a farming village outside of Hong Kong. Her parents violated the one child law and the woman who lived next to them said Fen was hers. She was unable to have a child.

She was five years younger than her brother. They lived in a small house, with flimsy walls and only one big room.

She was about four years old when an earthquake struck her village and the mudslide that followed wiped everything out. Fen and her brother survived only because they were out playing. Immediately she was an orphan, but instead of going to an orphanage, she and her brother lived on the streets. They slept in an old train car, ate by stealing food from the market, and made money by running errands and shining shoes.

They were so young, but she could have lived that way forever. Her brother took care of her. Until the day he was hit by a car right in front of her.

She screamed and cried. He wasn't killed, but they found out they were orphans and had no parents. A newspaper had a picture of her crying and a wealthy family adopted her.

She never saw her brother again.

Fen had been searching her entire life for him, but he was nowhere to be found. She wouldn't give up.

The sight of the boy in the green and blue shirt brought back fond memories of her brother. She watched him run off after leaving the treats for the soldiers.

She wanted to follow him, but the news reporter began and

she wanted to listen to make sure everything was relayed properly. He would be easy to find. He tucked himself against the corner pharmacy store watching the broadcast.

Fen waved. He waved back.

"The people here welcome the humanitarian efforts," the reporter said. "As you can see ..." She pointed behind her. "There is not the brutality that is being reported. There is happiness, gratefulness. The people of Mitton cheer the soldiers and the children play with them. They finally are receiving proper med—"

BOOM.

The loud explosion rocked the ground and a blast of heat caused a fast, high pressure wave of air that lifted Fen from her feet and threw her in the air and a distance of ten feet. She landed hard on the concrete, face down, knees first and catching herself with her hands, breaking the fall enough that she didn't smack her head off the ground.

There was a pressure-filled pain in her ears and they rang so loudly she couldn't hear.

A split second after she landed, she felt droplets, hitting against her hands like rain. Only it wasn't rain, it was blood and debris.

She sat up and everything spun. Her eyes rolled back causing vertigo to strike temporarily.

Was she hurt? She didn't know. It was hard to assess. She

tried to focus, but things shifted out of control, rolling from her vision as if she were drunk. Her hands moved on the ground, feeling her way around and her fingers hit something.

Looking down she saw it was an arm with a hand attached, a hand still holding a microphone.

All around her were body parts. Arms, legs, heads. It was a bloodbath. Parts of the store were strewn across the street, mixed with food items.

People screamed, but they were drowned out by the constant ringing in her ears.

It gave it a very surreal, dream like feel.

Fen tried to get her bearings, get it together. Giving it one more attempt to stand, she peered up and when she did, she saw the little boy still across the road. Again, he smiled at her and then he ran off.

Fen wanted to scream out in frustration, how could she be that stupid? How did she not see the explosion coming? She bent her legs, got her footing, attempted to stand, but a pain shot through her hip and she buckled back down.

*You're weak. You're weak*, she told herself. *Get up. Be strong.*

After one more attempt, she succeeded. More than anything she wanted to chase down the boy, but she couldn't. She'd have to order someone else to do it. Fen had to get it together, get her balance and take care of the situation at hand. A deadly situation she didn't see coming because she never expected it to happen.

An error she wouldn't make again.

# Caldwell, OH

The military phone was placed right where Troy had said it would be. In the feminine protection disposal box in the third stall of the old McDonald's. Cal wondered how in the world he would explain not only what he was doing in an old McDonald's, let alone the women's room. Sure enough, like everyone else, Cal was given light janitorial duty in the mess hall. Which was … McDonald's. He was to do that, stay busy until they found him more of a permanent job.

Because he wasn't American he had a different status there.

They didn't search him like they did others. He was able to conceal that phone in the waist of his pants.

He rested after he had arrived at Caldwell, and they gave him some sort of medication that actually made him feel much more energized.

Almost everyone had a job. A lot of the detainees were working at the Walmart cleaning shelves, packing items, and accounting for them. Cal had a bunk in a tent set up in the Walmart parking lot. But only those fully trusted or who weren't American weren't under lock and key after work hours.

There were two living areas.

For refugees, who were more like detainees, hundreds of tents, campers, and box houses were set up in a large fenced-in area within a fenced-in area that extended over the highway toward the prison. Once the detainees were allotted evening exercise in the free area yard they were placed in lockdown in their tents.

The Nobel Correction facility was the other living area, for those who were labeled prisoners of war. Those people didn't have jobs nor were they inside the actual prison. They slept like animals, outside, on blankets. The night before there was rain and the hundred or so of them huddled against the building to stay dry.

He hadn't the chance to speak to anyone yet, but Cal observed the routines as best as he could.

Refugees were treated more humane. As they filed out of their tents in the morning, they were given a protein bar, water and released to work. During the guard change in the afternoon, they were lined up, given a meager meal, and placed in the free area to eat and walk around. After an hour they returned to work until sun down. Same routine, a meager meal, and yard time. Only they were allowed to use the portable showers set up against the fence. The lines were so long many didn't get the chance to wash.

For the prisoners, it was different.

They were fed once a day and done trough style. The water in one, a slop in another. It was degrading.

Cal was fortunate. He and eight others ate in the mess hall after the soldiers were finished with their meals. He had fresh coffee as well.

He did wonder what the reasoning was that he had to put down he was an architect, considering his first two days he was scrubbing toilets.

A twinge of guilt struck him when he sat down with his lunch. His food was fitting and smelled good. It was some sort of beef with lots of vegetables and rice.

He was eating well, while others were not. When he was just about finished, a small laptop computer was placed in front of him, then a man in a button-down shirt sat across. He was one of the Chinese project supervisors. Those not military but had come over to aid in running things.

"Mr. Calhoun," he said in English but with an accent.

"Yes."

"I have received word that news of your exchange to your homeland will arrive sooner than we believed."

"That's great news, thank you," Cal said.

"In the meantime, this job of cleaning is temporary, but we have heard you are very brave."

"Me? Brave? I don't think so."

"You wandered the roads, faced radiation and scavengers all to try to make it to us and make it home. One of my soldiers has told me."

Cal wondered what soldier it was. One of the official soldiers or the Chinese American posing as one.

"Thank you," Cal said.

"We have a job that we need a man of your intellect and bravery."

It sounded big and important. Something that Troy would probably have screamed at him to accept.

"We have been lax and are far behind." He pushed the laptop to Cal. "We need to register every single refugee and prisoner in this camp." He flipped open the laptop. "The program is already available. You need to merely start logging them in. Can we ask that of you?"

Cal eyed the software, it looked easy enough. "Can I ask why you won't send one of your men to do this?"

"Because they need to go into the secure perimeter of the prison and refugee camp."

"Ah, they would have to be locked in," Cal said.

"It is safer for you than them."

What choice did Cal have? He agreed and after he was done with his lunch, he was taken by jeep the one mile to the Nobel correction facility where he was escorted into the fenced-in yard.

The guards carried a table and chair, set it up by the gate, then left.

Cal had previously been given instructions to interview as many as he could until the bell rung.

Once his table was set, no one bothered to look his way.

Cal stood and using a loud voice announced, "I am here like you are. Detained. I am taking names and information and putting it in a database so your families can find you. I know you don't want to but I ask that you do this. Or how else will anyone know what has become of you?"

"Are they really gonna let our families know?" someone shouted.

Cal shrugged. "No. Your families would have to seek you out. They have set up refugee search centers two hours every day in certain towns. They can check the database but if you aren't in it, they won't know." He waited for another question but one never came, and Cal took his seat at the folding table and propped open the laptop.

It didn't take long for the line to form. Cal glanced up to the first person in line. A young man, thin and frail who looked as if he was in need of medical attention.

"Name?" Cal asked.

"Tobias. Or rather," he said, "Toby. Toby Garbino."

## San Antonio, TX

Where was she?

"We will find her," Huang said. "She is in the area."

General Liu was fuming. He had just received disturbing numbers from his region on those infected with the virus. What he wanted to do was tell on her, call her superior and inform them she was out of control and her master plan was weak and was placing China in danger. She had no superior. Her uncle, the president, was her superior and there was no going to him. At least General Liu was one of the very few who knew that information.

Things had taken a turn in the previous few days, albeit small on scale, Liu could see them building toward something else.

They failed to secure the military leaders. They were out there somewhere. If the situation was reversed and the US invaded China, General Liu would be plotting his defense and resistance and would do so with an upper hand because he knew his own country.

He began his search for Agent Shu as soon as his reports were in. There had to be a mistake, he called the head of the bio defense division of the army, a man Liu had known and served with for years. His information about the weapon used didn't match up with the numbers he was seeing.

*"It depends what the distribution method was and how many places they left it,"* his friend said. *"This weapon is a supped-up version of Hand, Foot and Mouth. It is only deadly if the fever peaks or the sores get infected. It is however, debilitating for the patient. We*

*outlawed that weapon."*

Liu knew it was illegal, against rules of engagement which any good soldier followed.

Shu was not a soldier.

She was a weak-minded, power-hungry woman who wasn't going to secure victory. In Liu's mind, she was securing death for millions of people and not just Americans.

Sergeant Huang did not stay back as he always did, he stayed close, telling Liu it was because Shu was surrounded by agents when they found her in the office of the mayor.

"We are doing the best we can," Fen said to the mayor. "But our hands are tied, and help is limited until we receive full authorization. We won't get that until the surrender is secured."

"You'll never get the surrender," the mayor said.

"Then your people will die from this horrendous sickness."

General Liu stepped into her line of vision. Fen peered up. "Leave us," she said to the mayor. "And you, Sergeant," she spoke to Huang, "stay in the hallway."

When the room was cleared she slowly stood, walked over, and closed the door.

"One point seven million," General Liu said. "One point seven million Americans are on the brink of death from a virus that does not have that high of a fatality rate."

Calmly, she responded, "We need to help it along."

"That's just those dying, the number grows each day."

Fen shrugged it off and returned to the desk.

"The higher the number the more resistance will build."

"Just as I thought, you are here to chastise me when you should be doing your job."

"What job?" Liu asked. "Check on camps. I am concerned about the events here, the ones happening right now and the ones that will happen."

"The attacks?"

"Yes. Agent Shu, I implore you, as a military man and one who knows war, I implore you to send back the ships we have waiting in the ocean, return them to our homeland."

"Not with a second wave invasion imminent."

"We lost seven thousand men at the battle for the nuclear weapons center. Seven thousand with a new weapon we do not know of. In the mountain are military strategists who have access to everything."

"That mountain will fall."

"No, it will not. And the camps. The explosion you witnessed was one of fifteen. This is the start. Send our troops home to protect our homeland."

"You have no right to direct me."

"And you"—he raised his voice—"have no right commanding

189

troops without experience."

"You, old man." She stood and walked to him snidely. "You are confusing defense for rebellion and that is what this is, a simple rebellion. The Americans are spoiled. They are throwing a tantrum. We treat them well, what do they want from us?"

"Their freedom," General Liu said. "The loss of seven thousand men is not rebellion, it is a sign of a war. One you are not expecting. You do not know what you're doing and what is coming."

Slowly she walked to him, almost tauntingly and she stood toe to toe. "You present a façade of knowledge when you only fear the Americans. You are nothing but a sympathizer. We are here. We have them. And soon other countries will be on our side. You fail to see beyond your cowardice and you have spoken your final insult. You, General, have been warned." Without saying any more, she walked out, leaving Liu alone in the room.

## Mitton, TX

His name was Mason and he was smarter than the average eight-year-old, smaller, too. He had been given a complete set of instructions, but he didn't know why. He was told he was going to be a hero and that was good enough for him.

"Run," was the number one rule. "Run as fast as you can."

Then he was told to take the cupcakes to the foreign soldiers as a thank you. "Run after you give them the treats and go see Mrs. Stewart in the cake shop."

He did all that. But no sooner did he get to the cake shop, he heard the sound of an explosion.

"It's a good thing I came here," he told her. "I could have been out there."

"Good thing." She helped him change out of his blue and green stripped shirt, washed his face, then sent him out the back door to where his Aunt Trisha waited in a pickup.

"Did you see the boom?" he asked her when he got in.

Aunt Trisha nodded, said nothing, and drove quickly.

He wondered if she was mad.

Mason wanted to talk about the explosion, ask her if she saw it, but she didn't seem in the mood to talk. They remained quiet for the fifteen-mile drive to the farmhouse. She pulled into the driveway and stopped fast, making Mason snap forward.

"Go in the house," she instructed.

"But I want to see Uncle—"

"Go."

"Fine."

Aunt Trisha stepped from the truck and slammed the door. She moved quickly to the barn. Mason wanted to follow her, but he knew the barn was off limits, so he stayed outside and sulked.

Trisha shoved open the barn doors with a vengeance. Six men including Mason's uncle surrounded a table with boxes. There were also two trucks in the barn.

"You." Trish pointed.

A tall, strong-built man turned around. "Hey, sis."

"Don't *hey sis* me," she barked. "You made our nephew a messenger of death."

"I did no such thing. He delivered cupcakes."

"He could have been killed!" she screamed.

"He was fine, we had people watching."

Trisha growled at him. "When our sister died, we … you and me … vowed to take care of our nephew. To try to give him a life."

"And what kind of life is he going to lead in this world?"

"He is not a soldier, he is a boy."

"Everyone is a soldier now," he said. "He did great, and one day he will hold his head up and be proud he made an impact. Yeah, I'm sorry it was dangerous, but we got them today. They didn't see it coming. We almost got that Chinese chick that's running it. Plus, he didn't get hurt."

"Is that how you justify it? You did well and he didn't get hurt? How did this mind-set happen to you?"

"I always had it," he said. "It's stayed hidden since the service.

But when I was in New York and I saw it happen ... then the invasion, I knew I had to do my part and bring it out again. Using Mason was ... probably wrong, I should have asked you first. I promise you, I won't use him again. Okay?"

Trisha nodded. "Yes. Where now?"

"We are talking to a resistance outside of Ohio. They're setting up a coordinated attack. I'll know soon where we go next. In the meantime, go deal with Mason." He turned to walk away.

Trisha reached out and grabbed his arm. "All this. Moving every other day, always on the run, always fighting ... is it worth it, Sebastian? Is it?"

"Yes. Yes, it is," Sebastian replied. "More than you realize, this will work. Out there, everywhere, people are doing their part. It's the only way."

## Office of the Prime Minister, England

Adriene Winslet was furious. She was about as close to a temper tantrum as she could possibly be. She didn't need confirmation or intel to know what had happened at NORAD. It wasn't the Americans that killed all the soldiers and she immediately placed a call to Petrov.

"You went rogue. How dare you!" she scolded him on the phone.

"They called for help."

"There was a plan."

"Yes, there was, but we underestimated the force that remained. They needed help securing the command headquarters."

"It was not your call. The Canadians are in there, surveying. Right now, the People's Republic of China has control of the United States and commodities. It has been two weeks since we have received anything. Now with this, it will be even longer."

"This is nothing," said Petrov. "If we do not help the Americans counter and counter now, it will be a long time before we see any shipments from the United States. They have a massive fleet and movement toward the US for another invasion. Now is the time."

"I cannot commit the troops at this time. I have unprecedented discord right now. The troops cannot deploy."

"I don't want the troops, I need your resources."

"You went rogue, Mr. President. That was not part of the plan. I only agreed to help because our military leaders were going to pull a joint effort in coming up with a fool proof ..."

"Madam Prime Minister," Adriene's aid called her and held up a phone. "President Shu."

Every corpuscle in her body paused at that moment when she heard the name of the president of China.

"I will call you back," she said to Petrov. She hung up that call and took the phone from her aide. "This is Prime Minister Winslet." She paused. "Yes, Mr. President we are aware. I assure you we had nothing to do with this. Our resources are very strained and ..." Again, she paused as she listened, as the president of China did no less than back her into a corner.

# CHAPTER SIXTEEN

## Eighteen Days Post Bombs

## Caldwell, OH

Harris recognized that navy blue shirt with the green checkered pattern. He saw the man wearing it when they served food. He was envious, not from a fashion standpoint, but rather the man had an extra layer of clothes.

There were other colors mixed in the pile, brown, green, white … but seeing that shirt, the one he knew, told Harris that it wasn't going to be long before he died.

Something he feared.

He wondered a lot of things. Had they not chased the truck would they have been arrested? What if they stayed in the shelter just one more day? There were a lot of what ifs, but Harris would never know. The truth was he was captured for some reason, arrested for being a war criminal, and penned up like some sort of wild animal.

Each day, each hour that passed, those in the pen became animals. Daily fights broke out, and it didn't take long for people to go from refusing to eat the garbage they served to fighting over a handful.

No one really messed with Harris, he was a big man. Toby on the other hand wasn't and Harris did all he could to protect him. Even though Toby boasted he could take care of himself. His face was still swollen beyond recognition over the pummeling he had taken.

In fact, protecting Toby for the evening was how he saw the shirt.

Everyone searched for a spot to sleep, to eat their measly rations, go to the bathroom. Harris found a far-off corner of the yard. Where a concrete barricade had been erected with barbed wire to stop anyone from going behind the prison to the remaining yard.

He made a spot for him and Toby but soon realized why no one took that spot.

The smell.

There was a horrendous smell that carried outward every time the wind blew. Harris knew as the days passed that it would only get worse.

He couldn't see the source of the smell just by peering over the barricade, but when he walked to the very end where the barricade met the fence, and he pressed his face against the very corner, he could see not only what caused the odor but why they weren't in the prison.

Mounds.

In the rear prison yard were mounds of bodies, and Harris knew they were inmates. They had been killed, every single one of them, then discarded.

The piles were made up primarily of those jumpsuits the prisoners wore with occasional dots of other bodies with other clothing. Such as the blue and green checkered shirt.

Harris had just seen that man. He saw them take him out of the yard. The man wasn't any trouble, not a fighter, he was chosen to go.

As they all would be.

He looked carefully for purple, because that was what Marissa was wearing. They hadn't seen her since they arrived.

He didn't see purple anywhere in that mound. He'd check again later and keep checking.

*There has to be a way out*, Harris thought. With more prisoners in the camp than soldiers, there had to be a way to overturn things.

He was bound and determined to find that way.

"Hey," Toby called out groggily.

Harris looked over and Toby was sitting up. "Hey, you didn't miss breakfast." He walked to him.

"I'm not eating that stuff."

"You have to eat. Seriously, you have to," Harris told him. "Bet about right now you're sorry you lost that weight."

"Nah," Toby said. "I need to be nimble. I'm gonna get out of here and get us help."

"I believe you will," Harris said. "We both will."

"What about Marissa?" Toby asked. "If we get out, we can't leave her behind."

"We may not be able to take her with us but we will come back for her." Harris peered over his shoulder to the barricade. "If you know she's still alive."

"I wish there was a way to find out."

"Who knows." Harris sat down, and when he did, his eyes focused outward. "Wait. Maybe there is." He lifted his hand slightly and pointed to the guy they called the census taker. The man who came in with his little computer, spoke with a British accent and took down their names. He was leaving from his morning census, but he'd be back. Harris would ask him. He could know about Marissa. It wouldn't hurt to try.

<><><><>

At the rate it took to check in each person, with the amount of people in each camp, Cal believed it would take months.

He was allotted only a certain amount of time in the prison yard, less than the other area because those in the prison were considered extremely dangerous. Admittedly, Cal was nervous in there and around them. He fumbled so much he dropped things when he gathered his laptop and folders. Biscuits, crackers, and those little foil packs of peanut butter he saved from his meal for a later snack. He was just glad he never dropped that phone.

When they stopped him just outside the prison gate, he thought for sure he was in trouble for hoarding food. His heart raced and ears burned, fearing getting in trouble.

"Mr. Calhoun," one of the English-speaking supervisors said as he approached him. "A word?"

He pulled Cal aside.

"Look, if it's about the peanut butter ..."

"No. No worries, that is your food to do with what you wish. I have good news."

"Good ... good news?"

"Yes. Your government has just negotiated a deal for your safe passage back to your homeland."

"For me? Wow."

The supervisor smiled. "It is for many of you. There are tens of thousands of United Kingdom citizens here on holiday or business. Or were when things began. You will be returning to your country by ship. In a few days, we will transport you to the state of Virginia to board the vessel. While you are obligated to do so, we would appreciate the help with the data until you depart."

"Um, yes, sure. Absolutely. Thank you."

"You are going home." He walked away.

"Yeah," Cal said. "I'm going home." It seemed surreal, like a dream or some sort of trick. When he thought about that again, it hit him. He was there because Troy asked for his help. Cal didn't know when the liberation of the camp was going to come but he was willing to wager, he would be gone before it happened.

He still had to try to help. Before heading into the other yard to do his data work, Cal excused himself and went to the only place where he had absolute privacy … the porta john. There he was able to send a message to Troy. He would send him as much detail as he could, as often as he could, until he was no longer able to do so.

## Holly River Base, WV

It was surprising that he had any skin at all left on his face, that was how many times Steve had rubbed his hand over chin.

It irritated Gus, who looked up from the large table and huffed at him.

The base was empty with the exception of Troy and his team; they didn't have to leave early because they were assigned Caldwell.

"Of those in the area, we are locking down fourteen. That's close to fourteen thousand people, possibly more," Gus said pointing to the map.

"Where are we moving them?" Steve asked.

"Washington, PA. Untouched, no Procs there. Intel said it's too close to Pittsburgh so it's been left alone," Gus replied.

"Do we know how many people in these camps are infected?" Steve asked.

"No." Gus shook his head. "No, we don't."

"The infection is out of control," Troy said. "Millions have it, millions are dying."

"Yes, but"—Gus smoothed his hand over the map—"we have low infection rate here on the east. It's focused primarily in the Midwest and west. Which tells me that was where it was delivered."

Steve rubbed his chin again.

"What?" Gus snapped. "What now?"

"Well, what if they have it? What if a large amount of these people have it."

"Then they have it. We'll treat it. It's treatable," Gus said. "After phase two, camp liberation, then we send our men out to look for antivirals and antibiotics for the sores. Welch has been in touch with a team hunkered down in Fort Dietrich. They say it is treatable, they just don't have the means to mass produce."

"That's where we come in," Troy said. "After I liberate Caldwell and drop off the refugees, I am on a team headed to Dietrich. It's a rescue operation for those scientists."

"Speaking of Caldwell." Steve lifted the different sheets of paper with images. "I am not seeing a satellite of Caldwell."

"No, we don't have one," Gus said. "Our man inside stopped contacting when he turned over the phone to the Brit."

"What has he said?" Steve asked.

Troy replied, "Not much. He's not communicated much because he doesn't know much."

"From what he has sent us," Gus said, "it's the same as everywhere. They stupidly are routine. Same time slots every day they return all prisoners to the yard. Total of eight entrance guards at the camps. Sundays all prisoners are detained in camps."

"And like everywhere else," Troy added, "the camps are at least a thousand feet from the hub or main town where the personnel and soldiers are concentrated."

"Small team," Gus explained. "Each town. I don't know what the others are using to disable but the plan is the same across the board. We're using a nerve agent, heavily concentrated delivered in the town, at the same time we down the fences. Our troops then pick off the soldiers. Civilian casualties to the minimum."

"We expect runners," Troy said. "We'll chase them down. The plan is to get them all as fast as we can, keep it silent so word doesn't spread. Silence is crucial."

"What about other camps and towns?" Steve asked. "I know there are more out there than the ones we're hitting."

"There are." Gus nodded. "But if this phase goes well, then we will put a huge ass dent in their efforts. Game changing."

"So, this camp liberation is phase two? What's phase three?"

"Welch is working on it now," Gus said. "It's the biggie. If all goes well it will go down about the same time as these coordinated camp attacks or shortly thereafter. So much will be happening, they'll be chasing their tails."

Troy looked at Steve. "I know this has come together awfully fast and it seems rushed but is has to be. We have to do this before the second wave arrives or before they send them back. Right now, they're so vulnerable they don't even know it."

"As long as everyone follows the plan," Gus said.

"What do you mean?" Steve asked.

"I mean unlike the previous phases which only had a time frame, everything in this phase is coordinated and is to take place at the exact same time. All it will take is for one team to jump the gun and it could backfire with a devastating ripple effect," Gus said. "Let's just hope that doesn't happen."

# Swall, CA – San Joaquin Valley

When Joe found out Saul was ill, he was concerned. His friend looked bad and even though he tried to portray otherwise, he was quite ill. He ran into town to get Saul something but there was absolutely no medicine on the shelves of the stores. In fact, he couldn't buy anything in the store, everything was confiscated and taken to distribution.

He knew Mary Lou was close to a woman in town who worked with natural remedies, so he called her.

She was the one that told him about the new plague. Only it wasn't a plague, more of a virus that had been hitting other areas pretty hard and had arrived with a vengeance in Swall.

"I heard outside of Los Angeles close to a million are sick," Mary Lou said.

"That's just rubbish, ain't been nothing like that since the Spanish flu."

"I'm telling you, Joe. It's bad, even the State News Network is reporting it. If they're reporting it, you know it's out of control."

The State News Network showed a fifteen-minute news segment every hour. They were always bright and smiling, reporting things like citizens who are 'helping the cause.'

Mary Lou told him there was a hospital set up at the gymnasium at Farmersville High School. She had been placed on volunteer duty there on weekends.

Joe convince Saul to go. When he first took him, the ground of the school was clear. Only a few military vehicles were around, a few official tents and no more than a dozen soldiers. Inside he checked him in, then they found him a cot. There weren't as many people as Joe imagined. He believed Mary Lou was exaggerating.

Until suddenly his workers dwindled down to twelve, then six. Joe had a great visual of the severity of it when he stopped to see his friend on the way to drop off his quota one day.

The wide green lawn was completely covered with tents and cots, and inside there was barely enough room between beds for healthcare workers to walk through. There weren't that many of them.

They stopped Joe before he could go inside and told him it was far too dangerous.

"I'll wear one of those masks," Joe told them.

The refused. No one was to go in.

Joe peeked in the gym trying to see Saul, but he couldn't. Saul wasn't in the same spot as he had been the day before. The sounds of sickness were so loud, he had even heard it before walking into the building. Coughing, moaning, crying out. People moved a lot on their cots, probably trying to get comfortable.

"I'm just worried about my friend, is there any way to see how he's doing?" Joe asked.

The reply he received was, "Same as everyone else."

Joe left frustrated and angry.

He understood though and it was evident how bad Swall was hit when he went into the center of town.

Very few people walked around. There was no line at distribution and the drop off was empty as well.

For the first time, there were more soldiers on the street than Joaquin Valley citizens.

"Joe," Mary Lou called his name. "Hey."

Joe paused in unloading his truck. "I didn't see you at the table. I got worried for a second that you were sick."

"No, not me," Mary Lou said brightly. "I'll keep on going, you know me. The pierogi club keeps me strong."

Joe looked at her curiously. "Okay."

Mary Lou looked over her shoulder and reached to the back of the truck for a crate. "I know that back of yours is bad, let me help."

"What are you …?"

"No, Joe, I insist."

Joe wasn't quite sure how much Mary Lou thought she was helping to lift that crate, but it sure felt as if he were carrying the load and her hands were just placed there. He realized that was the case when he set the crate down and saw the blue card with his picture on it. He made eye contact with her.

"What's a travel permit?" Mary Lou said slightly above normal level. "Oh, those are for people who have to make cross-state deliveries. It allows them to get gas, you don't need one of those." She mouthed the words, "Take it."

Joe looked down at the index size card. Slyly, he pulled it to him as he reached for the last crate.

"Put it in the glove compartment," she whispered, then backed up. "There. Whew! Those are heavy. Come on I'll check you in."

She walked over to the table and Joe, as he normally did, brought the cases to the drop off door. With his dolly in tow, he walked over to Mary Lou.

She handed him the clipboard. "Sign, Joe. Give me the top and take the bottom for your records. You haven't been doing that."

"Must be something new," Joe said. He signed for his drop off, lifted the sheet to grab the one on the bottom, and paused.

"Take it. And don't forget, Sunday is a day of rest. I don't want to see you in town that day."

"Yeah," Joe muttered and looked at the sheet. It wasn't a copy, it was a delivery order for Fat Joe tomatoes to be dropped off in Ohio. More than the order form, the Post-it Note on top nearly made Joe's heart stop. The note read, "Toby's alive.

Prisoner. Caldwell, Ohio."

"Have a great day."

Joe handed her the sheet, then folded the order, closing his eyes for a moment. "Thank you. Thank you so much."

Mary Lou stood, leaned across the table, and kissed Joe on the cheek.

It took everything Joe had not to lose it right then and there. He took the dolly, loaded it in the truck, waved to Mary Lou, and then got in.

After placing that order on his seat, he removed the Post-it and crumbled it in his hand. He couldn't move or breathe, he was overwrought with emotions and gratefulness.

Toby, his only family member was alive and Mary Lou pretty much broke some serious rules to give him a ticket to go get him.

After pulling it together, Joe drove off. He was indebted to Mary Lou, more than she ever would realize.


## San Antonio, TX


While they fed her well, gave Madeline a clean and comfortable environment, they found a way to torture her.

It wasn't physical, it was mental.

There was a television in every single room, including the

bathroom. They all played the same thing all day long and straight through the night. Nonstop. She didn't have the ability to turn off the sets or even unplug them. The volume adjustment was manipulated as well. She could increase it but not lower it.

Snippets of BBC News showed rioting and fights in Europe, how a food shortage was breaking the country. There was news from other countries as well, though brief. However, for the most part, it was footage of what was happening in the United States.

None of it was good.

A computer-generated voice narrated the video images of United States citizens, starving, living, and huddling in destroyed buildings, children crying and injured. And the worst were the images and videos of those suffering with the new virus that was raging not only across the United States but the world as well. Patients on cots or lying on the ground, covered in sores, barely moving and struggling to breathe.

Sickly images all while the narrator said, *This is your country. Feed your people. Your people are dying. You can save them. There is no room for pride when it comes to the well-being of others. Come to us so we can help them.*

Adding to that, Fen Shu would come into the room four times a day and say the same things to her. Badgering her relentlessly.

"Give up. Surrender. Save your people."

Madeline would look away from the television. "Face that." Fen grabbed her chin and made her look at the footage of those sick with the virus. "Save them. Let us save them. Look at them. They are a few of many. Thirty million people have this. Thirty million could die."

Madeline lowered her head.

"It has spread that fast. We know how to beat it. Thirty million," Fen said. "Surrender."

Sadly, with each passing day that surrender looked more like an option than not.

Fen stepped from the hotel room and merely pointed at the door for the guard to lock and secure it. She fixed her blouse, lifted her head high, and walked down the hall.

Another agent waited for her by the elevator.

"Well?" he asked.

Fen shook her head. "Nothing. Not yet. Soon. I believe it."

"Then we wait?" he asked.

"No." Fen pressed the button on the elevator. "She needs a push. The Americans need a frightening message about this virus. Clean the western camps."

"All of them?"

"All of them." The elevator opened. "Now, if you'll excuse

me, I have another problem to eliminate." She stepped inside the carriage. "General Liu."

The elevator doors closed.

# CHAPTER SEVENTEEN

## Twenty Days Post Bombs

## USNORTHCOM, Colorado Springs, CO

The radio played like something from the days of old when families gathered around listening to stories and tales. Layered with static, the voice had a tin can sound to it, but its message was clear.

*Following the announcement that they are in the midst of government restructuring of the US, the People's Republic of China issued an apology for the delay in exports. Food supplies and aid export will resume within the week and they are reaching out to leaders of the world to negotiate terms in efforts to return to seamless commodity exchange.*

"Goddamn, mother fucking son of a bitch!" Welch tossed his empty mug across the room. It pissed him off even more that it didn't break. "Arrogant shits announcing they took over pretty much." His temper tantrum fell upon a quiet control room. "Get me Gilbert in Alaska."

213

A few seconds later, a specialist announced, "Gilbert is on."

"Gil," Welch called out. "You hearing this shit?"

"I just heard," Gilbert said over the speaker. "Did we surrender? Was there one?"

"Not that I know of," Welch said. "But with arrogance like this, I am betting it's not long until there is one."

"You think they're expecting one?"

"Oh, yeah, I think they know it's coming."

"So, what now?"

"Timing is still good," Welch said. "Word is out. I'm waiting on a response and a yes."

"What do you think?"

"I think intel is good, things are in order. I think you and the others should hunker down … I'm pretty confident. This is will be a go. And in two days, this whole war will look a whole lot different." Welch paused. "Thank God."

## Caldwell, OH

There was something intimidating about the big man named Harris, when he made his approach to the table. Cal had seen him before, he was always with the younger guy with the beat-up face. But the big man never made an attempt to register. Yet on this day, he not only made it to the table, he pushed his way through to get to Cal before the cut off. And no one argued with him. He brought the younger guy, Toby, with him.

"Name," Cal asked.

"Harris Clemmons."

"We need your help," Toby said. His voice was weak and cracked.

"I don't know what I can do," Cal said. "Are you ill? Hurt?"

"Duh," said Toby.

"I'm gonna stand here," Harris said, "pretending I am checking in and you are going to answer his question."

"How do you know you can trust me?" Cal asked.

"We don't," Harris answered. "I don't care."

"You know he needs medical attention," Cal said.

"He needs to eat," Harris said. "They feed us pig slop. He won't eat it."

"That's not important," Toby said. "We're looking for our friend. She came in with us. She's not here. We're worried. Is she okay? Sick? Dead?"

"She?" Cal asked. "I can tell you that all women are kept separate. I haven't registered any female deaths if that makes you feel better."

Toby exhaled in relief. "Yes, dude, it does. Are you able to check her name?"

"Yes. What is it?"

"Marissa."

"Marissa what?" Cal questioned.

Toby looked at Harris. "What's her last name?"

"I don't know. Shit."

Cal threw up his hands. "We search by last names. It won't even let me search first only. I'll tell you what, I'll look around. I'll see what I can find out. When I come back later, I'll let you know."

"Time's up!" a soldier shouted.

Cal shut the lid to his laptop. "I have to go." He stood and reached for his items, stopping things from falling, and that's when he saw them, the peanut butter packets. He inconspicuously grabbed them in his hand. "I will be in touch." He held out his hand to Toby in a handshake manner.

Toby hesitated but as soon as he connected hands with Cal, his eyes widened.

"Take them," Cal said. "It's not much, but it's food."

"Thank you," said Toby.

"Thanks, man," Harris said.

Cal nodded and finished gathering his things. There was one other matter to tend to.

A phone message.

He wore a large bulky sweatshirt that hung pretty far covering the front pockets of his jeans where he kept that military phone. It vibrated when he received a message. No one could hear it, but his testicles knew when a message was received.

Cal had been feeling the vibration the last few minutes of the conversation.

He paused on the way to the next yard to use the porta john. Inside, he grabbed the phone from his pocket and held it near the vent for light.

"Sunday Mass at two o'clock. Lose the phone."

Cal lowered his head in relief. If he understood the message, the liberation was going to take place the next day. Cal would be gone, but he would leave knowing he at least helped in some way.

It made him feel less guilty.

The message also gave an instruction, lose the phone, and Cal was happy to do so. Before leaving the porta john, he tossed it where no one would ever search … in the commode. When it splashed, he knew it was gone, and Cal walked out of the portable bathroom.


## San Antonio, TX

General Liu stood leaning in toward a long table in his office. Other military personnel including Sergeant Huang were there.

On the table was a large map of the area.

"We have a lot of manpower at these health camps," General Liu said. "We need to move some around. The sick aren't going anywhere. We have rebel activity up near Austin and our docks are getting hit daily down at Corpus Christi. Our men are tired. We have relief troops on the ships in the gulf. Let's move those men in. Focus on these rebel …" He stopped talking and lifted his head when the doors to his office opened.

Fen walked in with four of her agents.

"Agent Shu, what can I do for you?" he asked.

She tried to stifle a smile, but it was hard to do. She looked smug. "General Liu, you are relieved of duty."

"What?" he asked shocked.

"You were warned. You are charged with insubordination, sympathizing with the enemy, and treason. A field court martial has been issued. Evidence has been presented to our government leaders and you were found guilty of these crimes and you have been sentenced to death, at dawn, by a firing squad of your peers." She looked at the agents to the left and her right. "Arrest and detain him."

Sergeant Hung took a step toward Liu as they grabbed him.

"Sergeant," she called out. "You are his assistant. Do we need to investigate you as well?"

Sergeant Huang stepped back.

218

"Thank you. Gentleman, I will have a replacement tomorrow." She made eye contact with General Liu as he walked by her, then she followed, wishing the men in the room a good day, as she pulled the doors closed behind her.

## The Kremlin, Russia

He had given all that he had left of him. His time, his concentration, his heart, but Petrov couldn't sit on it any longer.

The time was at hand. It was time to make a decision and it was one he didn't take lightly.

Prime Minister Winslet bailed on him. She was onboard until the last minute when she stated her constituents didn't want to get involved and that she had citizens abroad that she wanted to bring home. When she did that, she opened up her harbor to receive goods from the United States. Not that it was enough to stop the chaos over food, but in Petrov's mind it was enough to keep England under China's control.

Winslet believed staying neutral and working with China was for the best. Or so she said.

It was what was best for the United States.

Petrov strongly disagreed.

China had finally admitted to the invasion and declared a strong victory.

There were still strong United States Military hubs out there. They had already successfully succeeded in disruption diversions, liberation of camps and releasing numerous small towns from the China stronghold.

It wasn't much, but it was more than anyone expected.

Petrov had been in touch constantly with the head of their resistance operation. Now the general needed him again, this time bigger, this time to make a difference.

Until he heard otherwise, until he heard of an unconditional surrender, he was going to believe that the takeover was still hostile, and the United States was in need and wanted assistance as General Welch stated.

The problem was, no one but Canada wanted to assist. Even they were limited in what they could do.

His generals advised against it.

"Do you know what this entails?" his head general asked.

"I do."

"Do you realize, the wrong move isn't going to help America? It can and possibly will destroy the world."

"This is going to destroy the world either way," Petrov said. "The question is do we sit idly by and wait or do something about it? Anything that can stop it. Even if we fail, we failed trying, not burying our heads. This is what they want of us."

"We know this from rebels. We don't know this from the

country. I don't get it," said the general. "If the terms are the same, if everyone else is negotiating, why are we being the black sheep?"

"If they can do this to the United States, what is next? Who is next?"

The general strained a smile on his face. "Sir, China is not trying for world domination."

"You don't think? They have the food, half the weapons in the world. If everyone accepts this, they are dominating." Petrov walked to his desk. "Take a look at the last intelligence from Canada."

The general joined him and reviewed the items on the desk. One of which was a large map of the United States.

"There are pockets of resistance according to Welch." He pointed to the map. "And these locations according to our Canadian friends are other locations that are rogue and fighting."

"Where are the enemy soldiers?"

Petrov smiled. "They are not spread out like wildfire, they are concentrated."

"Which makes it easier for us," the general said.

"I sent a memo to you with the detailed idea of what I think we should do in regard to the American general's request. How we should proceed."

"I received it and I responded that it was high risk."

"If it works, then it is worth it."

"If it doesn't, will you still say the same?"

"I must believe I would," Petrov said.

"Alright then," the general exhaled. "When do we move?"

"Now. Evacuate the major cities. Move people into the shelters, prepare for the worst," Petrov said. "Once they are secure … we begin. We end this, one way or another. You know what to do. Let us do it."

# CHAPTER EIGHTEEN

## Twenty-One Days Post Bombs

## Swall, CA – San Joaquin Valley

There had to be rules of the road, curfews, but Joe wasn't sure about what they were. There was martial law in his area, no travelling on the roads after ten or before sun up. He assumed it was that way everywhere. He had his delivery order for eight cases of Fat Joe tomatoes, that was all. He was pretty certain that if there was anything else he needed aside from the travel form and order, Mary Lou would have gotten it to him.

She made sure, in so many words, to tell him to leave on Sunday. Which made sense, if Joe drove straight through for twenty-four hours, without stopping to rest, he'd be at least a thousand miles away.

Just on the outside chance that they were searching for him and his travel papers were void, Joe prepared for that. Using what fuel he had remaining on his farm, he filled as many five-gallon square containers as he could. He placed them side down on the bed of the truck and covered them with the crates. He secured those with bungee and then placed his packed bag and supplies in the back seat of his truck. He brought water, food, blankets, and everything he could think of to survive in the mountains, should he and Toby need to hide out east. The final piece to go was his gun. He tucked it away under the back seat, praying as he did so that it would never be found should his truck get searched. By the time he was finished, the sun still hadn't risen. With a couple hours to go, Joe sat in his reclining chair and closed his eyes.

He fell into a deep sleep, woken by the sound of the ringing phone. It stopped by the time he had jumped up to get it. There was no caller ID so there was no way to know who called. One step away from the phone, Joe jumped from his skin when it rang again. Quickly, he answered.

"Hello."

Breathing. Rushed, shaky sounding breathing.

"Hello?"

"They're gone," Mary Lou whispered. She wasn't crying, but her voice quivered. "They're all gone, Joe. Dead."

"Who? Who is dead?"

"Everyone."

"Mary Lou, what's going on?"

"God speed, Joe," she said.

"Mary Lou."

Click.

She hung up and Joe put down the phone, grabbed his jacket and his keys, pulled the door closed to his house and hurried to his truck.

It was daylight. Joe needed to be on the road headed east, but for all that Mary Lou had done for him, he had to go into town to check on her. It was the least he could do.

## Caldwell, OH

Something was different. Toby had fallen asleep the night before finally feeling better and stronger. He only lost his balance now when he stood, instead of all the time. The guy, Cal, had slipped him two of those military MRE packs of peanut butter and Toby devoured them. He even had no problem taking a handful of water from the trough. He just had to put it out of his mind how many people's dirty hands reached in there. Including his own.

It was weird when Cal slipped the packages to him, he wanted to hug him, thank him, but he couldn't because he didn't want to get the dude in trouble. It gave Toby hope that all was not lost.

The protein, the peanut butter was what his body needed. For soul, mind, and body. It powered him up enough that when he woke up he was ready to work on that hole by the fence. The area by the body barricade, not even the soldiers went near there. A section a little over two feet long where there was a separation between the fence and ground. Every couple of hours, Toby would walk by, stare out and use his foot to push the dirt, then the next round, he would bend down, grab a handful of dirt and move on.

Eventually that hole in the ground under the fence would be big enough for him to slip through. Maybe not Harris, but Harris said that was fine. If Toby got out he could try to find help … if there was any to be found.

His mouth was dry when he woke up, which was typical because he was still breathing only through his mouth, and Harris wasn't nearby.

He grumbled out his daily, "Hey," and when Harris didn't answer, Toby grew concerned.

Stumbling to stand, Toby held onto the wall until he had his balance. He wanted to make his way to the one water barrel and grab a drink.

When he got there, the barrel was on its side and the entire area around it wet.

Someone had knocked it over. He bent down to touch it and his senses kicked in. He hadn't noticed it when he opened his eyes because it was always noisy, but on this morning, he heard the sound of trucks, lots of them, in the distance.

Within seconds he heard shouting, voices all meshed together, and he couldn't make out what they were saying. He looked up and that was when he saw what seemed like every single person in the camp standing at the fences.

Their arms were flailing, voices shouting.

The entire prison yard was empty, they were all there.

He spotted Harris standing in the back. He was hard to miss, he was so tall, and Toby made his way to him.

"Dude," Toby said.

Harris did a double take as if surprised to see Toby. "Hey."

"Why am I sleeping through everything?"

Harris shook his head. "I just walked over here myself."

"The barrel is knocked over," Toby said.

"Yeah, there's no water."

"At all?"

"At all. The soldiers came in and emptied it."

"Is that why people are shouting?" Toby asked.

"No. They're shouting because it looks like they're pulling out," Harris said. "Something is happening, we just don't know what and we're trapped in here."

Immediately, Toby turned.

"Where are you going?" Harris asked.

"We aren't trapped. My hole man, the one I have been working on. I can finish it." Toby made his way toward the hole.

"Toby. Wait," Harris called.

Toby didn't. He was excited. If the soldiers pulled out he could work on that hole without anyone stopped him. But as soon as he got there, he dropped down to the ground in defeat.

"I tried to stop you," Harris said out of breath. "They did this last night."

Toby shook his head. Not only was his small hole filled in, but a trench of concrete and rocks had been placed in the vulnerable area. Toby touched it, it was still damp, but it served its purpose.

The idea of escaping under the fence was snuffed.

Like Harris had said, they really were trapped.

# CHAPTER NINETEEN

## Swall, CA – San Joaquin Valley

Just before the Sundrive Gas and Go was the check point that Joe went through daily. While he was certain the soldiers there knew him, it was Sunday and a day Joe didn't go into town. He pulled out his identification and planned to be honest when they asked why he wasn't dressed properly.

A friend was in need.

He could have gotten to Farmersville High school faster and easier, but all the side roads and most access roads were blocked.

With the roadblock in his sight, Joe slowed down the truck.

As he pulled closer he wondered, where were the soldiers? The blockade gate was across the road, but the post where the four soldiers usually stood was empty.

Joe leaned toward the steering wheel, peering close to the windshield as he drove slowly toward the gate. He was so focused on looking for the guards, he never saw what caused the thump and jolt of his truck.

He ran over something.

Joe stopped the truck, opened the door, and stepped out. When he did his foot landed right on the body of a soldier.

Quickly, Joe jumped out of the way. He had run over a soldier; how did he do that? Unless he was already on the road.

Walking backwards, Joe moved away from the truck and he heard the buzzing of flies. As if in slow motion, he turned around. The guard soldiers were there, only they, like the one under his truck, were on the ground.

He stepped closer to take a look. He didn't need to be a doctor to know they were dead and that they hadn't been shot or stabbed. All of their faces were a pale shade of blue. Their lips and noses were purple, and a pinkish foam seeped from their nostrils and mouths.

Horrified of what he saw and frightened that somehow he would be blamed, Joe opened the gate and got in his truck and drove to town. He decided he was going to make a beeline to headquarters to report it.

Problem was, it was more of the same when he arrived in town.

Military vehicles had crashed, soldiers lay dead in the street and by the cars. Joe slowed down enough to look, now understanding what Mary Lou had meant by, "They're all dead."

Frightened for her, knowing she was scared, Joe made the left on Florence Avenue and picked up speed to the high school.

He stopped at the check point, but when he stepped from the truck, he knew he was able to drive right through.

The bussing sound of flies was loud, adding a backdrop hum that broke the eerie silence.

It wasn't more of the same. There were four dead Chinese soldiers, but unlike the others, they were surrounded by a pool of blood.

They had been shot.

Joe drove through and went as far as he could. The yard area was filled with tents and cots, blocking the driveway and Joe had to walk.

More dead soldiers and not a whimper, cough, or moan from those ill on the cots or tents.

Everybody?

At that moment, Joe stopped walking and he ran. He ran as fast as he could to the gymnasium building.

The doors were open and as he raced in, he nearly tripped over the body of another soldier. He was different. He wasn't riddled with bullets or sickness, he had been butchered. Stabbed so many times, his neck was nearly decapitated. When he looked away from the body, that was when he saw Mary Lou. She stood center of the gym, amongst all of the bodies on cots.

Every single body was covered.

Mary Lou raised a gun to her head.

"Stop!" Joe yelled out. "Stop."

Slowly she turned around. She was covered with blood. "Joe," she whimpered. "You're supposed to be gone."

"What are you doing?" Joe walked to her. "What happened here?"

Her lips quivered. "Our work is done. The others, they left, I just ... I don't know if I can live with what happened."

"What happened?" Joe grabbed her shoulders.

"They killed them, Joe." She looked around. "They killed all the sick. We were told not to come in for our shift yesterday. Then Sergeant Edmunds found me. They gassed them. They gassed every sick camp from here to San Jose. It happened last night."

"Jesus."

"I covered them. That was the least I could do."

"What happened with the soldiers?"

"It wasn't part of the plan, you know."

"What? The dead soldiers."

"No, the dead neighbors. Our friends, the sick, they weren't supposed to be killed. We didn't cause this. It was ordered from the top. Our plan was already in motion. It worked, too. We came in and took those who didn't die from it, we picked them off. Shot them …" She turned her head and looked elsewhere. "Stabbed them. All of the soldiers. All of them dead."

"Mary Lou, that's thousands."

"We only had to pick off a dozen or so. They were easy. They were panicking. Running, Screaming." She spoke dazed.

Joe gave her a jolt. "What happened to the other soldiers? How did you kill that many?"

Still, Mary Lou looked elsewhere, staring around. "Poison. Ricin. Saturday afternoon they were fed it, they were dead before sun up."

"How did you poison so many?"

Slowly, Mary Lou went from looking away to looking at Joe. Her eyes connected. "Saturday, they served the tomatoes to everyone."

Joe's hands fell from her. "My tomatoes."

Mary Lou didn't answer.

"How many of my tomatoes are poisoned?"

"They were never going to our people, only to the soldiers and their leaders."

"How many?" Joe asked.

"The workers have been poisoning them since day one."

"Oh my God." Joe stepped back.

"You need to go, Joe."

"What are you going to do?"

Mary Lou smiled. "I'm gonna go be with Greg."

"No, come with me."

"I can't. I don't have the travel permit and someone here has to look like the guilty party. I'm fine with that. But go. Go before news gets out that this happened."

He knew she had a point and with daylight in full force, Joe had to go. He nodded, gave her a look of gratitude, stepped back and then hurried out. He was barely through the gym doors and outside when he heard the lone gunshot.

He paused for a second, closed his eyes, then continued on.

Joe didn't look back as he pulled from the school, drove through town or through the road block. He'd figure out later what to do with those tomatoes in the back of his truck, obviously, they were tainted. The highway was empty, he didn't see a single car or military vehicle. He supposed eventually he would.

He kept going, never once looking in his rearview mirror, never once dwelling on what happened back home. He couldn't. Joe had to focus forward, move ahead and find his nephew, Toby.

Toby was all he had left in the godforsaken world.

That was his mission, his cause. Joe would get there, he'd find him, even if it was the last thing he ever did.


There was a moment after Joe left, when Mary Lou briefly gave a second thought to what she was about to do. She had led a good life. She thought about God and how He would view her actions. When she told Joe she didn't know if she could live with what had happened, she wasn't referring to the slaughter of the soldiers, *that* she could live with. It was the loss of everyone she knew, the loss of her freedom, her homeland. A part of her, in a sense, felt responsible for the sick people who had been gassed, her karma. They had already poisoned the soldiers; the ricin was working its way through their systems when they gassed the sick camps.

Mary Lou had never felt so much rage as she did when she received Sergeant Edmunds' call. She raced into town and joined the others in 'picking off' those soldiers who were not poisoned. The first enemy soldier Mary Lou saw was scared, she saw it in his eyes, and then she saw the red of rage as she lunged for him. He wasn't ready but she was. She repeatedly stabbed him mercilessly. She did it for her friends, her neighbors who were defenseless when they died.

Just like that soldier Mary Lou killed. He was one of three that she personally murdered.

She could live with that if she had to, but she didn't want to.

The war was far from over, but her part was done. She was ready to see her husband. Continuing what she was doing when Joe walked in, Mary Lou whispered a short prayer asking for forgiveness, put the gun to her head, and fired.

# San Antonio, TX

It was dark, hot, and the air was humid. General Liu had been stripped of his uniform shirt, jacket, and awards, left only in a T-shirt and pants. No shoes. He was placed in a basement room of a hotel. No windows, no light, only a few glow sticks.

No one came to talk to him, he was given no water or food.

He thought of his life. The service he had given his country, his daughters who were grown and in school, studying to be doctors.

The bright spot to it all was that he would see his loving wife who left him and the earth far too soon. He hoped that when word reached his daughters that they wouldn't be affected by the shame he caused them. He prayed that they knew him well enough to know their father didn't betray his country, he was doing what was right for the world.

His final moments on earth weren't filled with regrets, but loving memories of those he held dear.

When the door opened he knew it was morning … it was time.

They secured his hands behind his back before they took him from the room. His eyes had time to adjust as they led him down a lit hall to an even brighter hotel lobby.

He was taken out a back door through the kitchen to a small

secluded courtyard.

The sun beat down hard and the heat was extreme. They walked him to the center of the area. Fen waited before a line of five soldiers. One of which was Sergeant Huang.

General Liu looked at them all before being placed in position.

Fen dismissed her agents, then walked to General Liu. She spoke to him in a low voice, almost taunting. "You can only say so much before you are silenced for good. Now you stand before executioners of your peers."

"Only someone with a blackened heart would do such a thing to loyal men."

She laughed. "Loyal. They jumped at this chance. They know of your behavior as of late. How you want to help the Americans."

"We are here for the country, that includes the people. If we are to live among them one day, we cannot do so if the sins of our actions forever taint their perception of us."

"You failed to draw a line," Fen said. "Quite a shame you will not see the victory of your country."

General Liu shifted his eyes to her. "Neither will you."

"Any last requests, General?"

"Tell my daughters I love them."

"Very well."

"I suppose you will enjoy watching this," General Liu said.

"I will not be watching. I don't want the perception that this is personal."

"But it is."

She merely raised her eyebrows, then stepped back. "Would you like a blindfold, a covering?"

"No. I will go with my eyes open and standing tall."

"Very well." She walked away. "Sergeant Huang, once I am gone, you may do so. But do so quickly."

"Yes, ma'am."

General Liu tried not to look at her but caught her in his peripheral vision as she walked from the secluded area.

"Ready," Sergeant Huang called out.

Hands behind his back, General Liu stood straight.

"Aim."

He lifted his chin proudly, taking a deep breath. He would not leave this world scared, but rather he would do his best to be brave.

A split second before he hollered, "'Fire," Sergeant Huang stepped from the ranks of the line, pivoted his body and on his call, gunned down the four other soldiers.

General Liu was waiting for the bullets, but what he witnessed, shocked him so much, he dropped to the ground to his knees.

Huang lifted one of the rifles from a dead soldier, slung it over his shoulder and raced to General Liu.

"Sergeant Huang. You …"

Huang pulled out a knife and reached behind General Liu for his bound hands. "I have help with an escape plan. We'll go through the catering room, back to the basement. I need you to hurry." He cut the binding on General Liu's wrist.

"What you did, Sergeant Huang …"

Suddenly, he spoke perfect English, and Liu understood him. "My name is Tommy Cho." He helped General Liu to his feet as he spoke fast. "I am a First Sergeant in the United States Marine Corp. I am a plant. I think you're a good man. Come with me." He pulled on his arm. "Please"—he looked at him squarely in the eyes—"don't make me regret this decision."

Without any choice, and grateful for saving him, General Liu went with the young man.

## Caldwell, OH

Troy was almost there. Seventeen miles out from the town of Caldwell. His team raring and ready to go, he received a message on the secure line.

"Abort."

Troy had been in the service long enough to know that no mission is simply aborted with one word and no verification. He looked down to the military phone and replied. "Verification."

A second later came the response, "Lenny Kravitz."

"Password."

"AFZ1965REAGAN."

"Damn it," Troy nearly slammed the phone. He took a second and sent another message. "Why?"

"Compromised. We're out of sync. Caldwell will be next wave."

He bit his lip and shook his head. "Pull over," he told the driver.

Another 'blip' and Troy looked down to the message.

"Before base. Stop. Hit high ground. Look up."

Troy crinkled his brow at the mysterious message. The truck had stopped, and Troy stepped out. They were already on backroads. He began to look around.

"Captain, what's going on?" one of his men asked.

"Mission aborted, men. I'm told there will be another raid. Right now, we're out of sync. So, someone jumped the gun." He looked left to right until he spotted a large hillside. He then glanced down to his watch. The small compass indicated east. "That … over there. Anyone have suggestions how we can get there? We need to get to high ground."

"Why?" someone asked.

"I don't know."

"Saw a road turn off about four clicks back," a driver said. "Bet that will take us to high ground."

"Let's try it. Everyone back in. Let's go," Troy ordered.

They regrouped and reloaded in the trucks. That road was not the one, but they did locate another when looking at the map. Just about the time they were supposed to hit Caldwell camp, they were all on top of the large hillside.

"Okay, we're on high ground," a sergeant said. "What now?"

"I'm told to look up."

"Look up?"

"Look up." Troy's simple mysterious message implied for them to look up. On that hilltop, heads tilted back with eyes on the sky, they all did just that and waited.

## San Antonio, TX

*Resources are not just fresh food and water, it is shelter, medical care ... a cure. With the exuberant amount of available hands, the plentiful vat of resources, the finest medical treatment. It is in the best interest of this country to hand over control to the People's Republic of China. Tens of millions of people are in dire need of medical attention over this virus.*

*In a few minutes, you will bear witness to my proclamation of surrender. I do this not with a heavy heart, but with a clear mind and optimistic view of the future.*

Madeline rehearsed her script in the bathroom of her suite before it was time to go.

*Good morning. My name is Madeline Tanner. Many of you know me as Speaker of the House. During a domestic attack on our country, those ahead of me in succession for the presidency were killed, and I was sworn in.*

She didn't write it, it was written for her.

*We are blessed and grateful that the People's Republic of China was ready to step in to help. Yet, we have refused their help and that has placed us in a predicament. They are at a loss to fully deliver what we need.*

She hated the thought of delivering it but what choice did she have? The surrender was to be such a momentous occasion that it was going to be broadcast to every available citizen who could watch a television. Her makeup and hair were done by a professional brought in to see her that morning, and a tailor fitted her with a perfect suit, aimed to sooth and reassure the public. They were setting up a podium on the Riverwalk, complete with a table where she would sign her surrender with parliament leaders from China.

Madeline was to look happy about it. After the surrender treaty, she would be free to an extent. She was granted permission to watch the rebuilding and reorganizing along with the distribution of food and medical care.

She had a morning drink to calm her nerves and declined a mild anti-anxiety. Fully presentable, she was taken from the hotel by way of limousine to the park where she would deliver the speech.

Fen Shu rode in the front with the driver.

It was a painful ride, emotionally she wanted to run and hide. She hated herself for giving up.

"Almost there," Fen told her. "A few more moments. Many people are out wanting to see this. It is a glorious day."

It would be over soon, then she'd find a way to bury her head in shame.

A few moments later, something changed.

Fen's phone rang.

"Yes," Fen answered. Then after a pause, the typically cool and calm woman blasted a, "What!" then hurriedly rolled up the window between her and Madeline.

Madeline wasn't too familiar with San Antonio, she wouldn't have had a clue that they made an abrupt turn, had that window not gone up.

Suddenly the leisurely drive picked up pace and Madeline was sliding back and forth across the seat with every wild turn until the limousine came to a slamming stop. She shot forward into the seat across from her and banged her head off the corner of the interior window.

She felt the hard pain and the warm feeling on the blood that instantly rolled down her face. In a total state of confusion, she brought her fingers to the injury as she fumbled to get up and back on her seat.

The door opened.

"Out. Now." Fen reached in and grabbed her. "Hurry."

"What's going on?" Madeline asked.

Fen pulled her out of the car with force and Madeline tripped. Her knees buckled and she caught herself before she collided with the concrete.

With a tight grip on her arm, Fen yanked her up and that was when Madeline noticed people were running, yelling. Cars were screeching to a halt, crashing into each other.

"Move," Fen ordered, pulling her through the street, weaving in and out of cars. They headed toward a coffee shop. "In here."

Approaching the store front, Madeline paused when she heard the sound of gun fire. She turned to look over her shoulder and gasped in shock when a soldier with a parachute, landed in the street, then another.

She looked up.

The clear blue sky of San Antonio was peppered with hundreds, if not thousands of paratroopers dropping to the ground, and Madeline was positive due to Fen's reaction, that they weren't soldiers of the People's Republic of China.

## I-64, Fifty-Three Miles West of Norfolk, VA

Someone on the bus told Cal that if they had driven straight through they would have arrived in about seven hours. But it wasn't that easy. Just after six in the morning, the yellow school bus arrived. There were two people already on the bus when Cal and another man boarded.

There was a sense that they were no longer prisoners. They were given food for the trip, beverages. There were two soldiers on the bus, but they were told it was for their safety, especially with all the rebel activity.

They travelled south, then north again, hitting various camps and towns to pick up people. All of whom were going back home. It was a United Nations bus. By the time they picked up the final passenger in Charleston, West Virginia, there were twenty-five people in all. Not all were from the UK; some were from Spain, Germany, France.

Cal wondered with each stop they made, *Would this camp be hit? Would this one be liberated?*

He started to get worried as it pushed toward noon. He knew there was going to be a coordinated attack, he just didn't want to get caught in it.

But when it was announced Charleston was the last stop, Cal relaxed.

With every mile covered, the mood on the bus lifted.

Cal wondered what he was going home to. Surely, somehow, his home had to be affected by what had happened in America. Were they on the brink of war or would Cal sail across the ocean to an unscathed UK?

He didn't have any details and no one offered much of an answer as to what the voyage would entail or how long it would take. Just that when they arrived, they would board the ship. He spent a lot of time staring out the window, watching the mile markers as they cruised down a barren highway.

A part of Cal was excited. He felt as if he had been rescued from the nightmare. He couldn't wait to get home, find his family and friends. Hold them in gratefulness. He didn't look the same as when he left. In the short time he'd been gone he'd not only lost weight, he'd lost his hair. The doctor at the camp told him it would grow back.

Someone on the bus shouted out, "Just saw a sign. We're almost there."

The bus cheered, then in a few seconds, came to a grinding and screeching halt. The stop was so fast that the tires squealed, the bus slid sideways, and items and people flew about.

Cal shot out his hands catching himself before he plowed face first into the seat before him.

Everyone shouted, questioning what was happening.

Cal looked up and saw the driver and the soldiers running from the bus.

"What the hell?" Cal said outload.

"Where are they going?" a person shouted.

"What are they doing?" people asked.

Cal stood as he made his way up front and looked out the window. The soldiers and the driver were running fast and into the wooded hillside.

Cal pushed his way to the front and followed three others off of the bus. The others followed.

There wasn't a car around, not a soul or sound. Cal stood in the middle of the road, baffled. The others surrounded him and were behind him.

Cal was in his own thoughts, one world, trying to figure out what to do.

"They keys are on the bus," someone said. "Maybe we should take it."

"They ran for a reason," said another voice.

"He was on the radio," someone said behind Cal. "I couldn't understand a word of it."

"Were they warned about something?" asked another.

"I don't know. I couldn't understand."

"Maybe it's a trap."

"Oh my God. Look."

Cal heard that and spun around. When he did, everyone was staring up.

The moment Cal lifted his eyes upward, his soul felt as if it left.

The cloudless blue sky was the perfect canvas to the white chemtrails of the rockets that streamed in perfect unison westerly above their heads.

There was no way to tell where they were headed and where they would land. All Cal knew was that he wasn't going home.

It wasn't over. Not for him, not for America, and not by a long shot.

# About the Author

Jacqueline Druga is a native of Pittsburgh, PA. She is a prolific writer having penned over a hundred titles. Her works include genres of all types but she favours post-apocalypse and apocalypse writing.

You can find more about the author:

Facebook: @jacquelinedruga

Twitter: @gojake

Website: www.jacquelinedruga.com

*No Man's Land* by Jacqueline Druga

When Leah and Calvin found out they were expecting, they were over the moon. That day would be one to remember forever…but for more reasons than one. That was the day the world changed. That was the day joy turned to fear. A deadly virus broke out, with many of those infected becoming violent and uncontrollable. And it was spreading fast.